Rough Cut

EDWARD GORMAN

Rough Cut

A MYSTERY

ST. MARTIN'S PRESS / NEW YORK

Library of Congress Cataloging in Publication Data

Gorman, Edward.
  Rough cut : a mystery.
  I. Title. II. Title: Rough cut.
PS3557.O759R6 1985   813'.54   85-2548
ISBN 0-312-69360-5

First Edition

10 9 8 7 6 5 4 3 2 1

For my favorite people, in order of appearance:
Mrs. Bernadine Hixenbaugh, Danny, Julie, Joe,
Hixie, Ben, and in loving memory of my father.

And for Carol, forever.

Special acknowledgment to Max Allan Collins
for much more than just the title.

I heartily disliked most of the advertising
agency persons; although I had a few friends
among them, I wouldn't have wanted to take a
blood oath with one.

—Bill S. Ballinger

He felt the loyalty we all feel to unhappiness—
the sense that this is where we really belong.

—Graham Greene

Rough Cut

ONE

As the lights went down in the screening room, the sweet, weedy aroma of marijuana rose from the back, near the projection booth.

There are a lot of holdovers from the flower-power days in our advertising agency. Invite them to view a rough cut of our new commercials and they think it's like seeing *Fantasia* back in '68.

The projector completed an exceptionally bad day for me by breaking down midway through the leader, throwing the room into darkness, catcalls, and a few giggles.

As if the day hadn't been bad enough. I was still considering swallowing a few dozen sleeping pills because of what a certain sleazy private detective had told me a few hours ago.

The house lights came up. The dozen people scattered throughout the movie-theater seats looked like escapees from the world's last disco—trendy to a fault. Many of the guys were dressed like cowboys to reassure themselves and others that they really were manly, while others were got up in less obvious but no less goofy costumes—short ties, pegged pants, sport coats that looked like bellhop jackets, even a few white-hunter numbers, apparently made necessary by the dense vegetation that Harris-Ketchum Advertising finds itself surrounded by here on the eighteenth floor of a Loop office building.

A few of the ladies were no less ostentatious. This fall the fifties look was back. Some of the women looked like chorus girls in a production of *Grease*. Fortunately, the majority were sensibly dressed and their looks didn't suffer a bit.

At the moment I was the only guy in the room with a regulation Wembley necktie on, and a suit that Richard Nixon would approve of. I am Michael Ketchum, forty-one-year-old partner in one of the city's most prosperous agencies.

At least that was true for the moment. Given what the private detective had told me, I had some serious doubts about our future.

The door to the screening room opened up and a kindred spirit walked in, a slight man in a dark brown suit. He looked like the sort of guy who ushered at church on Sundays and spent his leisure time building playthings for his kids. Except for his haircut, that is. He had one of those fancy razor cuts that belongs only on a Vegas lounge singer who uses his finger like a pistol when he wants to point out somebody special in the audience. For forty-four-year-old Merle Wickes, the haircut was all wrong: flashy to the point of being comic. It did not go with his jowly face or his beagle-sad eyes or his defeated little mouth. It was like putting Continental hubcaps on a rusted-out Chevrolet.

Merle came down the aisle and seated himself a few rows back from me. When we made eye contact, he glanced away nervously. Merle and I did not speak often these days. As far as he was concerned, the Harris-Ketchum agency had only one real boss—Denny Harris, the same guy who had transformed Merle's formerly traditional haircut into something that Wayne Newton would think was swell. Harris had transformed many other, less obvious things about Merle, too.

At least that's what the private detective had told me.

2

*   *   *

The commercials the writers tell you about, and that the art directors show you in storyboard form, are almost never the commercials you see in the screening room.

In the studio or on location, things happen, things change. An actor has trouble with a line, so it must be rewritten or altered in delivery so much that it carries a different nuance. Then there's the editor. He or she thinks that the third scene should go where the script calls for the second scene. So that gets changed.

Et cetera.

By the time you sit down in the screening room, you're likely to have a different commercial from the one you scripted. Sometimes the changes lift what was a mediocre commercial into something special. Sometimes the changes turn a thoroughly enjoyable, if unpretentious, spot into a piece of incoherent gibberish.

The lights went down.

The film flickered on the screen again.

What appeared there for the next thirty seconds was a prime example of incoherent gibberish.

The lights came up.

It was obvious from the faces that my cursing had been audible throughout the screening room.

Everybody stared at me. Waiting for me to speak—to tear into Ron Gettig, the producer, who sat in the rear. He was one of the guys wearing a jungle jacket and toking on a joint. He was also one of the guys I always kept in mind when I was working out three times a week in the gym. The thought of him kept me moving around the weight room, getting myself in shape for the inevitable day when I smashed in his smug, Marlboro-man face. He only looked tough. In a bar one night a small man he'd insulted had made quick work of his nose. He'd deserved and gotten a bloody face and a reputation as an empty bully.

Immediately, people started leaving the screening room, calling out the names of the bars where they could be found over the next few hours. It was autumn and early dusk made the trek to waterholes seem all the more urgent. By the time Merle Wickes left, knowing what was coming, seeming anxious about it, only Gettig and I were left.

He had his size 12 feet, encased in snakeskin cowboy boots, propped up on the back of the seat in front of him. A cheroot was in the corner of his mouth. He upped the ante by putting amusement in his blue eyes.

Once a year I went to management seminars where consultants always pushed the same point. Deal courteously and patiently with employees. Give them the benefit of the doubt, even when you're seething inside. Ask questions and listen sympathetically to answers.

"I'm really tired of your bullshit, Gettig," I said, standing over him.

Two days ago, when I'd seen a rough cut of this particular spot, I'd pointed out to Gettig that the ending was wrong for our marketplace, and our particular consumer. I'd told him I wanted the ending reshot. Instead, he gave me the same ending, only edited in such a way that the offensive scene played an even larger part in the commercial.

But you don't know what I'm talking about, do you?

Traynor Chain Saws is this agency's largest account, spending an average of ten million a year on television, radio, and print advertising. Without the Traynor account, we would be half our size and a very mediocre agency. There was even a good possibility that, if we lost the account, we would be perceived as being on the skids, and the rest of our clients would seek help elsewhere. Clients like to be associated with winners, and an agency that's just lost half its billing hardly looks like a winner.

4

The Traynor account is special in another way. It appeals to an older demographic of middle-middle-class (and upwards) craftspeople. The Traynor costs more than any other saw but the Traynor customer doesn't mind spending it because he knows it's worth it.

Now, you can probably deduce from what I'm telling you what the average Traynor customer is like. Over forty, financially secure, a man who takes quiet pride in his work, whether he uses it to make a living, or just cuts off an occasional branch in his backyard.

He is not your beer-commercial macho type. Any gusto he gets comes from professional pride.

Yet it was the beer-commercial machismo that Gettig kept giving me. The last scene showed an overly muscular sweaty guy cutting down a tree with enough grimaces and groans to fill a half hour of professional wrestling.

The guy may be somebody Gettig is related to, but he was somebody who would offend the average Traynor customer.

Gettig stood up. He's six three. I'm five nine. He hoped to intimidate me. He didn't.

"I'm taking you off the commercial," I said. "Giving it to Molloy."

"Molloy," he sneered. "He says eek when he sees a bug."

"He's a good producer."

"Meaning he takes orders," he said.

"Meaning he does what's appropriate."

He grimaced, much as the man in the commercial had grimaced. Then he leaned toward me a bit. "Maybe someday I'll do what's appropriate."

"Get the hell out of here, Gettig."

We were both starting to lean toward each other when the door opened and Tommy came in. He saw what was happening and his young Norman Rockwell face—complete with curly blond hair and freckles—got tight.

"Shit," Tommy whispered loudly enough to hear, as if

he'd just stumbled between participants in a western gun battle. He glanced longingly at the door, obviously wishing he could put himself in reverse and get out of here.

Most people around the agency liked Tommy. I wasn't quite sure I did. He was a college intern, a twenty-two-year-old trying to learn the agency business so that when he graduated in a year he could have a job waiting for him. He worked hard, all right, but there was something nervous and a little sweaty about him for my tastes—he was always finding ways to remind you of how hard he worked, and he could butt-kiss shamelessly, praising a piece of mediocre ad copy until it sounded like a sonnet of Bill Shakespeare's. The only thing that redeemed him in my eyes was the fact that he wasn't very good at all the political games he tried to play— his failure giving him a vulnerability that kept him likable. He was given to a lot of "Gee's" and "Goshes" and the hell of it was, despite all his puppy-dog careering, you knew he meant them.

"Is everything all right?" Tommy asked, coming down the aisle. He knew things weren't all right, but he also knew that simply by asking the question, he could interrupt us and calm us down.

Gettig opted not to take the opportunity for a truce. He turned to Tommy and sneered, "Things'll be all right as soon as Mr. Vice President learns that Denny Harris gives the orders around here."

"Meaning what?" I snapped.

"Meaning I screened the spot for Denny and he liked it fine."

If Denny Harris had okayed the spot, then what I planned to do in half an hour was going to be even more of a confrontation than it already promised to be. It only increased my rage.

"Aww, you guys," Tommy said. "It's people my age who're supposed to act like that."

6

"The Little Drummer Boy," Gettig said sarcastically.

"He's right," I said, calming down. I paused. "I suppose we're being a little less than professional."

"I like the spot. I've got no apologies to make," Gettig said.

"As I said, I'll take it up with Denny."

"Yeah," he said, "you do that." Gettig looked up the aisle at the door. "I've got an appointment." He nodded a chilly goodnight and left.

I turned to Tommy. "Sorry Gettig and I are such jerk-offs. Great role models, aren't we?"

He smiled. "I understand. Psych's my major."

Now it was my turn to leave. "See you tomorrow."

"Yeah. You be good to yourself."

In the twilight gathering in the windows employees threw on scarves, hats, heavy coats. You had the impression they were about to face the Arctic. Actually, it was still above twenty degrees outside. I said maybe half a dozen goodnights, then went into my office, grabbing my phone messages and taking them along with me. Probably more than in any other profession ad people are surgically attached to their phones. When clients need you, they need you.

None of the calls looked especially urgent, so I allowed myself the luxury of sitting with my face in my hands and calming down from my scene with Ron Gettig. He was typical of the tension in the Harris-Ketchum offices—part of the staff was loyal to Denny, the other half to me. That the larger share belonged to me wasn't as comforting as it should have been—Denny had enough true believers to make life up here, at least on some days, really miserable.

Glancing at my watch, I lifted the receiver and quickly dialed the number of my personal accountant, Tony Hauser. Tony himself answered. "Hi, I was about to call you," he said.

My stomach did some unpleasant things in anticipation of

bad news. Given what the private detective had told me, I didn't see what could be any worse.

"You find anything?" I asked.

"Boy, you sound wound up."

"Just had a bad scene."

He laughed. "Why don't you get one of those honeys I always see walking around up there and tell her you need to relax—if you know what I mean."

Like too many people, my friend Tony believes that because ad agency types occasionally work around models and actresses, we're always spilling our seed. Unfortunately, that's not generally true. Denny Harris, my partner, being an exception to that particular rule.

"So," I said, wanting to get it over with, "did you find anything out?"

"Not yet; that's why I was going to call. Kind of a progress report."

"So you haven't had any trouble geting in?"

"Not a bit. I may take up burglary."

For the past three nights, thanks to master keys I'd given him, Tony Hauser had been sneaking in up here and going through the books.

Denny Harris and I shared a genuine bond of trust, as you can see.

Tony yawned. "I'm a little tired, though. I mean, working from midnight till three isn't my idea of a good time."

"Well," I said, thinking of what lay ahead of me, "keep me posted, will you?"

He laughed again. "Hey, relax, Michael. What's the worst thing I could find out?"

"That the bastard's robbing me blind."

He chuckled. "You got a point there."

I hung up and leaned back in my chair and let my eyes roam the chain of electric lights spreading across the city below. You reach a certain age, or state of mind, and what

8

you find yourself doing is clinging—clinging to things that you once would have scoffed at as mediocre, things that are now embarrassingly important. Stokes, the private detective I'd hired, had already told me some of the things Denny had been up to. On my own, I'd come to wonder about how Denny was handling the business end of things and whether my investment was safe. Mediocre to worry about retirement, which is not, after all, a very romantic subject. But I was of the age, clinging, maybe too tightly, to the few things I could call my own.

In minutes it was my turn to bundle up against the waiting cold night. I dressed just as excessively as everybody else. All I needed was a damned husky to complete my getup.

All the way out there I planned what I was going to say to Denny, and just how I was going to say it. In my mind it was a speech equal to Churchill at his best. The only difference was that mine had a few more expletives.

9

TWO

Ten years before, Denny Harris had taken what was left of a once-large inheritance and bought himself the kind of stone-and-wood home Hugh Hefner probably dreamed of about the time he was buying his first box of Trojans.

Situated on a tract of land that lies somewhere between the suburbs and the country, Harris's home is hidden by deep stands of fir trees on both sides. It is an ideal rendezvous for a lifelong bachelor whose only pleasures are alcohol and other men's wives: there are no neighbors in any direction for at least half a mile; Chicago is several miles away.

Wind promising snow whipped the firs as my headlights speared the driveway. The double-stall garage doors were closed. A Mercedes coupe sat in the drive. I cut the lights, afraid that I recognized the car.

The lights in the house were out. As I left my car, pulling my collar up as I moved, I thought I saw something blur in the second-floor window but I couldn't be sure.

I knew I was being watched. Probably they thought it was amusing, my coming out here this way. Denny always likes portraying me as old-fashioned and unhip. Coming here was the sort of thing that would give him good material for cock-tail chatter.

Before going inside, I tried the Mercedes's door. It was open. I leaned in and looked around for the registration. It was in the glove compartment. It did belong to the person I'd suspected.

My stomach knotted painfully. Tonight I would forgo booze in favor of Di-Gel. At least if I wanted any sleep.

I went up to the side door of the huge house—Denny refers to it grandly as his estate—and knocked. I knew it would do no good. They would hide like children in the shadows, giggling, and not answer my knock.

I tried once more, figuring I owed conventionality this much.

Then I tried the doorknob. It was locked.

I used my gloved hand to smash in a quarterpane of glass on the door.

The wind swallowed the sound.

I reached inside and unlocked the door.

I listened carefully for any voices, then went in. I felt sure they weren't laughing anymore.

The house was impenetrable with darkness. Only the kitchen window to my right held any light, the thin silver light of a winter moon. The house smelled pleasantly of spices and wood burning somewhere in a fireplace. I walked into the kitchen and stood still for a time and listened. All I heard was the house creaking and groaning in the wind.

I went deeper inside, past a fancy dining room at one end of which was a grandfather clock that toned the quarter hour severely, into a living room with built-in bookcases and the kind of leather furniture I'd never been able to afford, even before my divorce.

Nothing.

Shadows created by the fire in the walk-in fireplace danced from every corner of the room and played like slippery kids across the floor. The books were an impressive army of leather-bounds, show books in perfect condition, with names such as Socrates, Melville, and Proust on the spines, which was hilarious, if you knew Denny. He had once complained, earnestly, that *Playboy* was no longer fun to read because there was too much of a text-to-picture ratio. Unlikely that he spent his evenings perusing Galsworthy.

There was only one place to look. Upstairs.

At the west end of the room was a sweeping staircase that disappeared ominously into darkness. I stood and stared at it. I was, without quite knowing why, afraid.

The silence and the wind and the loneliness of the location were getting to me. A thin sheen of sweat covered my body and my pulse hammered faster than was pleasant. I was a kid again, facing not a bully as easily dismissible as Gettig, but something more inexplicable and terrifying—the imaginings of my own mind. God knew what lay upstairs. It was a much easier world when you could call out for your mother and father in the middle of the night.

I started up the stairs with what I would not call an impressive first step—I tripped and grabbed the banister. If there were ghosts or demons, they would be laughing their collective asses off at the moment, and I couldn't blame them.

I think I spent around an hour and a half going up the staircase. At least it seemed that long.

The higher I went, the darker it got, until I seemed to disappear inside the shadows, become a part of the night itself.

Creaks and groans of wood and glass and stone went off like little alarms every few seconds, causing me to jerk or jump or start every other moment.

Finally, I lay a shoe on the hall that ran the length of the second floor. Neil Armstrong couldn't have felt any prouder when he first set foot on the moon.

The first door I opened was the bathroom and I hate to break the mood here and tell you that, intrepid searcher that

I am, I quit searching and took a pee—but that's exactly what I did. Fear had filled my bladder.

I decided to forget about good manners. I didn't flush the toilet. The sound of it exploding would have been too much in the tense silence.

The second door I tried led me to a guest room. I had stayed in it one night while my divorce was finishing up. Denny had had a kind of bachelor party for me, complete with a woman who was his gift to me. I was too drunk and lonely to turn her down. I took her gratefully, waking up in the morning to find that she was all the things hookers weren't supposed to be—gentle, tender, bright, with at least a passing interest in my marital grief. I supposed I would have pursued her if I weren't the jealous type. The idea of her with innumerable men would have driven me crazy. My wife had had only a few lovers—at least that's how many she'd finally admitted to—and that had made me crazy enough.

Despite the ornate woodwork and the expensive appointments, the room had a sterile feel. Too many visitors had robbed it of its personality.

In the moonlight, I searched the room; closets, under the bed, corners. I had no idea why I was doing this, or what I was looking for.

No conscious idea, anyway.

But the guest room turned up nothing.

I went back to the hallway and pushed into another door. This one looked immediately promising. This was the den. Half the furniture in it was turned over or smashed. The contents of desk drawers were strewn all over. Any ideas I'd had about walking in on a simple case of adultery were now long gone.

I reached down and righted a straight-backed chair. Then I picked up some cushions and put them back on the couch.

The obvious motive for such a mess was robbery—or looking for something hidden. But somehow I didn't think so, especially when I felt the cold air seeping in and saw the smashed window. There was an air of purposeful violence about the room, somebody enjoying the task of destroying it, down to overturning the wastepaper can.

But ten minutes later I knew no more, so I moved back to the hallway, toward the one room I should have tried in the first place.

The master bedroom.

As I heard my footsteps creak on the floor, I thought of the form I'd seen in the window when I'd pulled in.

As a kid I'd enjoyed ghost stories. Boris Karloff had made a nice, safe spook. The kinds of ghosts I was likely to meet at my age were far more frightening.

He was sprawled across the bed, his blond hair silver in the moonlight, clad only in his underwear, blood in splotches across his back and arms as if someone had daubed it on with a paint brush. The white bedspread was a mess, blood in puddles.

The closer I got the better I could see the puncture wounds in his back. There must have been a dozen of them, each oozing.

A peculiar fascination came over me. Sickened and afraid as the scene made me, I was somehow riveted by it. Which was why I kept moving nearer. Only the smells his body had made in the aftermath of death slowed me down.

I kept moving toward the bed and what seemed to be a sheet of typing paper beside the corpse. Just as I drew near the corner of the huge bed, I thought how many husbands in this city would envy me the privilege of seeing Denny Harris this way. Hundreds of husbands. Literally.

I leaned over the bed and grabbed the paper, the reality of the moment real enough suddenly that I avoided looking at the body on the bed. All I could wonder about was where the

14

other body was—the one that belonged to the Mercedes downstairs.

Somewhere in the house, for sure. With a knife in her hand and blood on her arms like a surgeon after a morning's work?

The note was so crude and melodramatic it made me laugh, easing some of the tension that was threatening to make me crazy. Whoever had written it had seen too many Agatha Christie movies.

Beneath a blotch of blood, which lay in the center of the page, were typed the words, "NOW IT'S YOUR TURN."

I was literally laughing, faulting the killer for style (face it, advertising people are slaves to surface things) when my nose reminded me of my dead partner on the bed and the wretched, messy, reeking way he'd died.

This time when I stared at the note in the dim light, it no longer looked melodramatic, but rather ominous, conveying that same psychotic edge that Charles Manson brought to his killings—blood as symbol, blood as portent.

It was this type of unlikely rumination—maybe I'd do a little essay on murder for the local Op-Ed guest editorial column—when something akin to a tree fell on my head.

Coldness rushed through my nostrils and into my system. Whoever hit me muttered something, and then I was gone, literally and utterly gone, to some pained level of being that was not quite life and not quite death.

Presumably, the lady whose Mercedes coupe sat in the drive had found me—Cindy Traynor.

THREE

By the time I came to, the blood on the back of my head had had time to begin scabbing a little. That was the only way I could measure how long I'd been out.

In the moonlight Denny still lay sprawled ghostly pale in death, dark tears in his body.

I had no desire whatsoever for heroics. I didn't give a damn if she waited in the shadows watching me. I just wanted out and away.

I stood up, without much self-confidence, my head hammering, my eyes having trouble focusing, my bladder filling again, and somehow made my way out of the room and down the hall. The stairs I had to be extra careful with— didn't want to take a tumble down those. I used the banister judiciously.

The driveway was empty. She'd gone.

I stood in the frosty night, sucking in air, listening to distant animals settling in against the cold, and to a forlorn train punishing the darkness.

Finally, I got into my car, turned on the heater full blast, and backed out of the long drive.

I knew where I wanted to go, whom I needed to talk to. At

the first sign of a phone, I'd find the address and head there promptly, knowing that soon the police would be involved and I would have to have a story prepared.

The first phone I came to was attached to a convenience store that stood like a monument to plastic civilization in an otherwise rambling section of fir trees. When I got out of the car, I was dizzy a moment and staggered. The effects of being struck on the head were still with me. I saw the kid behind the counter in the store look at me with a mixture of pity and superiority. Obviously he thought I was drunk.

Inside the store, the lights bothering my eyes, I went to elaborate lengths to prove I wasn't bombed. But I moved so self-consciously I probably only looked all the drunker.

I wrote down Stokes's address—this was far too important to trust to a telephone—and went back out into the night.

Back in the city I found the expressway that would take me to Stokes's neighborhood. I drove toward it like a homing missile. I felt so many things—horror and fear, regret and a terrible nagging sense that somehow Denny had gotten what he'd deserved—that actually I felt nothing; I was really blank as the city rolled by on either side.

I had taken Stokes's name from the Yellow Pages when I'd first contacted him three weeks ago. I hadn't wanted to ask anybody for a recommendation because then they'd be curious as to why I'd wanted a private eye. But now—as I left the expressway and pulled into a neighborhood ashen with factory soot and a bitter sense of its own demise—I wondered if I shouldn't have gone to one of the big, prestigious investigative agencies. The neighborhood clarified many things about Stokes. He was a tall, fleshy, ominous-looking man who usually wore black. His thick glasses gave him the look of a comic-book World War II German spy. It made sense coming from this part of town, with its whispered white ethnic secrets and its battered pride and its obvious hostility. He

17

would take pleasure from prying into the lives of people like Denny and myself, and feel a power over us for knowing what we were really all about. For the first time I realized that I should not have hired Stokes, but the day I saw the note indicating that Denny and Cindy Traynor were having an affair, I'd gone a little crazy, thinking of all the things Denny was jeopardizing. So I ran my finger down the list of private investigators and chose him simply at random.

And now here I was—in so deep I had to turn to a man I didn't trust for advice. I had the feeling that Stokes would know what to do, had the feeling that Stokes had lived on the edge of the law all his life.

It was an old two-story frame house that had once been white but for over a decade or two had evolved into gray. An unlikely red neon sign burned in the gloom, announcing FEDERATED INVESTIGATION SERVICES. I supposed in a neighborhood like this one he got many calls. I parked and went up to the door.

Three knocks brought me nothing. I looked past the front door and across the screened-in porch to a lace curtain beyond which a small color TV glowed. I made fists of my hands to keep the knuckles from freezing, then pounded again.

I guess I'd been expecting Stokes. The tiny, shawled old lady who hobbled out looked like somebody central casting had designed to be in sentimental Christmas commercials. Except for the eyes. Even in the darkness there was a glow to the eyes that unnerved me—something brutal and selfish and hostile in their blue fire.

"Yes?" she said, smelling of warmth and scented tea.

"I'm looking for Harold Stokes?"

A surprising tartness came into the voice, the bitchy edge making her seem much younger. "So am I, as a matter of fact. He's two hours late. He hasn't brought me my treat tonight."

"Your treat?"

"Why, yes," she said, "my son Harold is a good boy. He's brought me a treat every night since he was a little boy." She frowned. "Except for the few months he was married, that is. The woman never approved of him doing that—so he stopped." She shook her head. "She just didn't understand how much Harold loved me, I guess. She seemed very surprised when he told her he wanted to divorce her and move back with me."

Great, I thought. Just the kind of private detective I want to get involved with. A mama's boy. I sure knew how to pick 'em.

I fished a business card out of my pocket and handed it over to her.

"Would you have him call me as soon as he can at my home number?"

"I'll be happy to," she said, "as long as he's finished bringing me my treat."

"Right," I said. I nodded and moved down the stairs as quickly as I could.

I was in my car—becoming aware of how badly I needed a drink—when I saw a red Mazda fastback in my rearview mirror. I recognized him by his hair—the Las Vegas hairdo Merle Wickes affected thanks to the influence of Denny Harris.

Wickes parked down the street, then walked back and up the same steps I'd just left. I slumped down in the seat.

He knocked on the door many times before the old lady came out. I must have put her in a bad mood. Her voice was scratchy and irritable as she informed Merle that her darling son Harold wasn't here.

Merle left, shaking his head, seeming extremely agitated.

I sat up and watched him move his pudgy body quickly down the street and into his flashy car—once again, Denny-inspired. For several minutes I rested my chin on the steering wheel, staring blankly out at the neighborhood.

How the hell did Merle Wickes know Stokes, the private detective I'd hired?

FOUR

I don't know how long I drove around, or what I saw, or even why I was driving. Every few minutes I would become aware of how my leg twitched, or how a shudder would pass through me and make a momentary spastic out of me, or how an uncomfortable sweat coated my body.

Of all the possibilities that lay before me, not one of them promised a welcome fate.

There was a possibility that I would be blamed for Denny's murder. We hadn't gotten along, I'd been out to see him shortly after his death (but would the police believe me that I'd found him already dead?), I might even have been seen leaving his place.

Then there was the possibility that the Traynor account would be leaving the agency and my financial well-being with it, a well-being heavy with various responsibilities . . .

From a 7-Eleven store I bought a six-pack of beer and from my coat pocket I bought some relief with two Valiums. I rode around long enough to feel the tranks start to work on me and feel fatigue dull the edge of my anxiety.

After my divorce, and before I felt much like falling in love again, I spent many evenings alone in my bachelor apartment feasting on Stouffer's frozen dinners and using self-pity the way other people used drugs. I also got into the habit of approximating a sensory-deprivation tank by sitting in the bathtub, throwing back several gins, and coming dangerously close to dozing off in the hot water.

Which is where I was three-and-a-half hours after somebody knocked me out at Denny Harris's house.

The lump on the back of my head did not throb quite so painfully now, nor did my jaw (I'd landed on it). I credited the healing process to the miracle wrought by the combination of hot water and cold gin I mentioned. Only this time I wasn't trying to deprive my senses; I was trying to use most of them in an effort to formulate a plan.

I suppose I could get smarmy here and tell you that seeing Denny lying there dead had made me have second thoughts about him, but it didn't. Like some others in advertising, he'd been a superficial, self-indulgent, lazy cipher who'd prospered on the talents of others and hadn't even had the honor or vision to understand his own parasitic role. He really believed he had something to offer other than hand-holding and racist jokes on the golf course for clients who appreciated such. His loss—sorry, John Donne—did not diminish the human race a whit. In fact, the species was probably the better off for his passing.

What might well be diminished, however, were the coffers of Harris-Ketchum Advertising.

The choice I faced was this—call the police like a good citizen and tell them where to find the body or simply do nothing, let the body be found in its own way, by the person the gods or whoever elected.

The reason the second alternative was appealing was because I would then not have to discuss with the police the identity of the woman who drove the Mercedes that had been parked in Denny's driveway.

Her name was Cindy Traynor. From what the private detective had told me, she and Denny had been having an affair for three months now. Cindy's husband was Clay Traynor, president of Traynor Chain Saws.

It was unlikely he would keep his account with us once he learned that his wife had been having an affair with Denny, and that I was implicating her in a murder charge.

Accounts tend to go elsewhere under circumstances like that.

As I rolled into bed in pajamas fresh from the laundry, I took an Arthur C. Clarke novel from the nightstand. Science fiction is my escape. But for once the sentences held no magic for me.

I turned off the light, smoked half-a-dozen cigarettes until the moist nicotine on my lips began to taste salty, and then made the mistake of trying to sleep. I'm sure you're familiar with the process. Getting entangled in the sheets. Dozing off for a few minutes at a time, then waking up pasty and disoriented, as if from a nightmare. Trying to keep your mind blank while keeping it filled with trying to keep your mind blank. Insomnia is one of the few reasons I can see as legitimate for suicide. Enough sleepless nights and anybody would put a gun in his or her mouth.

My life pushed in on me like walls meant to crush. I had responsibilities—three kids to help raise, two of them soon to be college-bound, and a father in a nursing home who twitched at World War II memories. Between the kids and my father, I was always desperate for money, overdrawn too many times a month, sweaty on the phone with the nursing-home people when my payments were late. Given Denny's behavior lately, I was afraid I'd let down the people who depended on me and the thought of that made me crazy in a way I couldn't cope with. My old man had worked thirty-five years in a steel mill without letting his family down even

23

once. I had no right to be any easier on myself . . . and at my age, starting over in the agency business was impossible.

I don't know what time it was when the city sounds seemed to recede—the distant ambulances less strident, the buzz of traffic less steady—or when I finally fell down an endless well of blackness into sleep . . . but it was wonderful whenever it happened.

Which was when, of course, the phone rang.

It had to be somebody who really wanted to talk to me, because the phone rang fifty times before I finally disentangled myself from the covers and located the source of the ringing.

I smashed the receiver of the phone to my ear and muttered something like hello—vaguely worried, now that I was waking up, that maybe something was wrong with one of my kids—when a female voice, breathless and a little drunk, said, "I didn't kill him, you've got to believe that."

That was when I started looking for a cigarette. Fortunately, I'd left them on the nightstand. Once my awkward fingers discovered how to make fire—you take the match head and you drag it across the slate and nine times out of ten the darn thing bursts into flame—once I got the lung cancer stirred up in my system and realized the call didn't concern my teenagers, I felt much better.

Then I realized whom I was speaking to. Or, more exactly, who was speaking to me.

Cindy Traynor.

"I know you saw me there tonight, Michael."

"Uh."

"I just want you to know I . . . I didn't . . . I wasn't the one who . . ."

All I could think of were the puddles of blood on the bed. And the way she'd slugged me from behind. Difficult to tally the nice, breathy voice on the other end of the phone with such carnage—but it was.

"You really hit me," I said.

"Did I hurt you?"

"Not permanently, I guess."

"I'm really sorry. I just got scared. I wanted to leave the house without you hearing me."

"I didn't hear you, believe me."

I thought of her classic blond good looks—the sort that belong in evening dresses of the formal sort in country clubs of the snootiest type. But there was another quality to her I'd always liked, a gentle refinement, almost a melancholy, which is why I'd been almost shocked when I'd found out she'd spent time with Denny. She seemed much, much better than that.

"He was going to dump you, wasn't he?" I said.

An odd laugh rang down the phone line. "Michael, I'm afraid you don't understand my relationship with Denny very well."

"So he didn't meet somebody new?"

Denny usually had a married woman somewhere on the horizon. The private detective had said that Denny had stopped seeing Cindy as often, but he wasn't sure that Denny had a new woman.

"It doesn't matter and that's what you don't understand."

I paused, the weight of the evening crushing in on me. "If your husband finds out where you were tonight," I said, "we're both done for." Then I got curious. "Where are you calling from?"

"My home. Downstairs."

"Clay could be listening."

"He's passed out. Drunk." She paused. "I really didn't kill Denny," she said.

I sighed, had another cigarette. Maybe, from what I knew about psychology, she really didn't think she had killed him. Maybe she was repressing it.

"OK," I said, unable to keep the disbelief out of my voice.

"Really."

"All right. Really."

"You don't believe me."

"I'm not sure."

"May I see you tomorrow?"

"For what?"

"For—maybe you can help me."

"To do what?"

"Deal with this. There's nobody else I can confide in. I'm sorry." She sounded rocky.

I sighed again. "When?"

"For lunch." She sighed. "After you've finished seeing my husband. He said he plans to spend the morning in your offices."

I had forgotten about that. Every third Thursday of the month, Clay Traynor came to our offices to look over new ideas—and to get his ration of bowing and scraping. He had a big appetite.

"My fingerprints," she said. "They're going to be all over Denny's house."

"If you're not implicated in any way," I said, then stopped myself. I was thinking about the private detective I'd hired. He knew what was going on. When he found out that Denny was dead, what would he do with the material he'd collected the last couple weeks? Go to the police? Use it to blackmail both Cindy Traynor and me?

"What's wrong?" she said.

I told her.

"Oh, God," she said, "I've been followed all this time? Why would you do that?"

I told her about the note I'd found by accident one day in the conference room, a lovey-dovey number from her to Denny. It was too flirtatious to indicate anything but an affair, even though it was ostensibly nothing more than a thank-you note for a party he'd given. That's when, terrified

26

that he'd lose us our biggest account, I'd put the private detective on him.

"God," she said, "it's so humiliating, being followed like that." She began to weep softly. In the sound of it I heard a deep but inexplicable grief. "My whole life's such a mess . . . I . . ."

"Cindy, listen—"

"No, I understand. You were only doing what you had to do. It's just having somebody spy on you . . ." The weeping again. "I think we'd better forget lunch, OK? Good night, Michael." With that she put the receiver down softly.

For a long time afterward, I heard her soft voice in my mind. It represented a curious peace in the ugliness of the night. I wanted to see Cindy Traynor very badly.

FIVE

"Two days. I don't understand it," Sarah Anders said to me the next morning.

I had walked down the hall from my office pretending to be looking for Denny Harris.

Sarah—a matronly, attractive woman in her late forties, and a woman as sensible as she is compassionate—is the private secretary shared by both Denny and me. Of course, she's much more than a private secretary—she tells us what we need to do, makes sure we do it, and occasionally even gives us ideas for improving our client services. Part of the reason for her knowledgeability is that she has worked in every department in the agency and knows the shop in detail. Probably, truth admitted, better than I do. I've never been convinced that copywriters, which was what I was originally, make the best executives. Nor art directors.

"Two days," Sarah said again, her shining dark eyes staring through the open door into Denny's empty office. Sarah was one of the few people who found virtues in Denny. Despite a lot of evidence to the contrary, he appeared to be redeemable—at least to Sarah. "I'm worried."

"You try his house?" I asked.

She nodded. "Every hour. It was the same way yesterday. No answer."

"He wasn't here at all yesterday, either?"

"No."

Yesterday had been so busy, I hadn't noticed. I was used to my partner's being gone for long stretches—usually trying to pretend he was somehow attending to business—so I never had any accurate sense of just how much time he spent in the office. I'd just as soon not know.

Which was when I caught myself—that thought. The present tense.

I thought of Denny on the bed. The puncture wounds all over his backside, as if somebody had gone at him with a pickax.

"Damn." Sarah slammed the phone down. She'd tried his house once again. She shook her head, perplexed. "I've tried everywhere—bars, health clubs. I just don't know what's left."

I had to play it as I ordinarily would. I put a smirk on my face and said, "Maybe he's found some new female delight to lose himself in."

For the first time, the worry line on her forehead looked less severe. She always got sentimental about Denny's affairs—though she would have been just as upset as I was about Denny and Cindy Traynor, like a mother considering her bad little boy. "He sure does all right with the ladies, doesn't he?" Then she caught herself and flushed. "Oh, sorry."

"It's all right." I waved a hand to my office. "I'll be in there working. If Denny doesn't show up, just show Clay Traynor into my office. I'll handle him till Denny gets here."

There: I had laid all the planks I possibly could so that I could act genuinely surprised when Denny's body was discovered. The dutiful partner, the hard-working businessman, the-show-must-go-on-vice-president—oh, I was a hell of a guy.

Waiting for me on my desk was last month's profit-and-loss statement. Denny took no interest in any detail—just how much we'd earned or lost. I spent more time with the statement, looking for any way we could save money and thereby increase our individual cuts. With teenagers and a dying father, I needed all the help I could get.

The P & L didn't tell me much except for one thing—the client-entertainment-expense column was still swelling up. Denny felt he had the right to write off virtually every dime he spent as a legitimate client expense—he hadn't paid for his alcoholism in years—even though he was literally taking it from my pocket. I owned fifty percent of the agency.

If I really wanted to make this look like a typical day, then I'd have to go down the hall to the accounting office and raise a little soft hell with Merle Wickes, the man with the Las Vegas haircut. Once a month I demanded to know why Wickes let Denny get away with it.

My intercom buzzed.

Sarah. "I'm going to call the police. Just have them run out to his house and check and see if everything's all right."

"You really think that's necessary?"

"Yes, I do." She sounded absolute.

What the hell, I thought. May as well get it over with, the discovery of the body, the inevitable questions of the cops.

"Well, OK," I said.

"Thanks, Michael," she said.

We hung up.

"I need to talk to Merle a minute," I said to Belinda Matson, the Accounting Department's secretary, an hour later.

As always of late, she looked unhappy to see me. There had been a time a year or so ago, when she'd first started working here, that I'd had notions about the two of us getting together. Sometimes she brought her lunch and one day in the lunch room I'd seen her reading Steinbeck's *In Dubious Battle*, a novel whose union theme made me curious about her. I'd asked her about it; she'd said that it had been her favorite novel in high school—she hadn't gone to college—and that she reread it every so often. She was a tiny woman, always pressed and fresh-looking, with a subtle kind of eroticism I found appealing. I'd had my share of fantasies about her—but as the rift between Denny and me widened about his spending habits, she began to see me as the villain who always whumped on her boss, Merle Wickes.

"He's in a meeting right now," she said. "But I'll tell him you stopped by. Would you like him to call you?" Pleasant, competent, and protective of Merle.

I stared at her blue, blue eyes. She was, I sensed, the kind of woman I needed, but I had no idea how to go about it. "Read *In Dubious Battle* lately?" I said, embarrassed by my lame approach.

Without missing a beat, she said, "Not lately, I'm afraid." Then she turned her head toward Merle's open office door.

Which was when I raised my head and saw a woman slap Merle Wickes hard across the mouth.

Belinda saw it, too.

Both of us froze, not knowing quite how to respond.

The woman who had slapped Merle was his wife, Julie. A pretty, dark lady of thirty or so, she spent most of her days tending to their retarded son. She usually looked tired—which made her prettiness even more impressive. Today she looked tired plus angry and embarrassed. She turned away from her husband—who stood there stunned—and walked toward me. She was one of the few employee wives I felt really close to. We tended to sit by each other and talk and laugh a lot whenever there were agency functions.

Now, she came abreast of me and touched my arm. "I'm sorry about this. I . . . couldn't help myself, I guess." She was right at the point where she was going to explode in either tears or anger or both.

I put my hand on her shoulder. "I'll walk you to the elevator."

As I spoke, I watched the line of her vision. She wasn't glowering at Merle this time. Instead her gaze was fixed laserlike on Belinda, who had her head down and was blushing.

Merle, looking devastated, glanced at me, then at his wife, then at Belinda, then closed the door quietly, as if he did not have strength to slam it.

I tugged Julie away and headed her toward the elevators down the hall.

Halfway there, she started sobbing. I put my arm around her and guided her along as best I could. Employees in the hallway mugged a variety of stares, even a few sniggers. This, in advertising, was the stuff of legend.

I got Julie on the elevator, then waited till the doors closed. Then I punched the STOP button. An elevator between floors seemed like a good place for privacy.

I let her cry until she shook. Occasionally I held her, then let her push gently away. Finally, she said, "I take it you know about it. I suppose everybody does."

"I'm sorry," I said. "I don't know what you're talking about." Though I had a terrible feeling I knew what she was going to say.

"His secretary, that Belinda, they're having an affair."

Of course, I didn't want to believe that. If it were true it would make me feel naïve, and not do wonders for my ego, either. I considered myself more appealing to women than Merle Wickes was. "Maybe you're just imagining it," I said.

"No," she said, starting to cry again, "he told me about it. Last night. He, he . . . said . . ." She started to choke on her tears. "He said that he loved her." She shook her head in disbelief. I could sympathize. I'd heard similar words from

32

my own wife one night. They were the worst words in the world.

So it was true, then. Curiously, I felt betrayed, too, as if Belinda had owed me something. I thought of her pert face and clean bobbed hair. She could have played an earnest mom in any number of TV spots with cakes and pies in them. She didn't seem the type to—

"But I don't blame Merle," Julie was saying, starting to dry her eyes now. "I blame Denny Harris. He's the one who got Merle to change the way he lived . . ."

Much as I had disliked and disapproved of Denny, that was one charge I couldn't agree with. The temptation rap was a false one. True, a year ago Merle Wickes had been a cliché of an accountant, a man who'd brought his lunch in a paper sack replete with grease stains, who spent his off-hours attending accountancy seminars, and who was inextricably bound up with the fate of his wife and his retarded son. Then he'd changed, begun hanging around after hours with Denny and Gettig and the rest of the fast-laners in the agency. His Las Vegas hairstyling was emblematic of that change, and of how he'd pulled away from his wife and child . . .

But was Denny to blame? I didn't see how. The desire and the will for such a change had to be within Merle in the first place. Denny only gave that desire shape . . .

"I hate him!" Julie said.

The anger in her eyes was terrifying. Because it was more than anger—it was some kind of deep dislocation. "He took my husband from me and my child!"

She grabbed my sleeve and started yanking. She had started sobbing again. "What will I do, Michael! I'm not strong enough to be alone! I'm really not!"

I had a terrible, uncharitable thought as I stared at her. I did not think of her grief, or of her wan, anguished child— all I could think of, watching her wild eyes and hearing her curses, was to wonder if she could have killed Denny Harris.

*　　*　　*

Clay Traynor appeared in my office door one hour after Julie Wickes had left, dressed in a red-and-black-checked hunting shirt, a wide, hand-tooled belt, designer jeans, and hunting boots. He was tall and angular and looked like a model for the L. L. Bean Company. In his hand he carried a white Stetson that he tossed dramatically across the room to my desk. It landed with a bounce across my coffee cup. Traynor studied me with his Nordic, good-looking face, testing me to see if I would show annoyance that he'd nearly spilled Brim across several final drafts of scripts. I didn't, of course. I'm a good adman and good admen know how to secrete local anesthetic so they can deaden appropriate nerves.

"Your partner," he said. "Seems he's still out playing." He laughed his big bear laugh and came into my office. He had played soccer in college and he still enjoyed a brawl. Clay had inherited the Traynor business from his father. He had a beautiful, faithless wife and a stadiumful of friends who drank his drinks and indulged his whims and privately considered him a fool. Throwing his cowboy hat across a coffee cup like Buck Jones was only one of a thousand irritating habits he had cultivated. He didn't have much else to do.

That he was also an hour late seemed not to bother him. At least he didn't mention it.

As he dropped himself in the leather chair across from my desk, I saw that up close his face did not look nearly as self-confident as his getup. A long night with booze had given the eyes a suffering cast and the fingers that barely perceptible twitch that can foreshadow permanent nerve damage. Which, in his case, was entirely possible. His younger cousin Ron actually ran Traynor. Clay was simply a figurehead, a man who divided his time between chasing waitresses and making his advertising people miserable.

To show you the kind of guy I am—obviously superior to

34

a bastard like Clay—four months ago I'd gotten up at his birthday party and proposed a toast to him. And I hadn't stopped there—no, sir. I went right ahead and made a little speech that compared him favorably with Socrates, Babe Ruth, Mother Teresa, and General Douglas MacArthur.

"Made you mad just then, didn't I?" There was a smirk in his voice, but for some reason it was halfhearted. Usually he could get me angry quickly and totally. Today there was something almost pathetic about him, like a pitcher in a slump throwing his best strike-out pitch only to get it knocked out of the park.

"When?" I said, trying to sound surprised and unaware of what he was talking about.

He leaned over and retrieved his hat. "My hat. I could've spilled your coffee all over your desk."

"Oh, that," I said, shrugging it off. "Yeah."

"I could see it in your eyes. You were pissed. No doubt about it." Stalking is one of his favorite games. He was stalking me now. But why?

"Your partner always puts up with me. Maybe now it's your turn."

The way he said it—so sharply—jarred me for a moment. The curiousness of his remark about maybe it being my turn made me stare at him.

Did he somehow know that Denny was dead?

But then I remembered him saying much the same thing to Merle Wickes one afternoon at lunch—something about abusiveness working all the way down the pecking order.

Obviously, the thought of Denny back there bloody and dead in bed was starting to take its toll. I hadn't realized it until now, but at least a part of me had been in shock for many hours after my discovery.

"You still with me, Michael?" Clay was saying.

"Oh, yeah, sorry. My mind was drifting, I guess."

He held up his Rolex as if it were a prop in a TV commercial and tapped it. "Maybe he's visiting the VD clinic downtown. Some of those chicks he spends time with—" He laughed one of those laughs that made me part of an in-group joke.

It wasn't a group I wanted to be a part of. I'd been alone long enough. I wanted a wife, maybe another kid. I didn't want to know any women who spent time with people like Clay or Denny. They were all members of the same leper colony . . .

"I hope you've got some great ideas for lunch," Clay said. "I'm fresh out."

I was just about to suggest a new seafood restaurant when the scream came.

I didn't have time to get across my office threshold before the screaming became much more serious—became the kind of eternal, baleful sobbing you hear during wartime when mothers learn their sons have been killed . . .

SIX

"Can I get you some more coffee, Mr. Ketchum?"

I put my hand over my cup, shook my head. In the past two and a half hours since Sarah Anders had screamed, I'd had five or six cups and my nerves were shot.

I'd already talked to Detective Bonnell, the officer in charge of the investigation, and I would have to talk to him again. Soon. He had come directly to our offices from the murder scene and was interviewing the people closest to Denny.

Sarah's call to the police had worked. They'd found Denny's bloody body with no trouble.

"You want a sandwich, Mr. Ketchum? I'd be happy to get you one."

"Tommy," I said, "sometimes you get me down."

He flushed instantly. He looked terror-stricken. "I do, Mr. Ketchum?"

"Yeah, like right now." I was unloading a lot of my own griefs and anxieties on the kid, but I did not give a particular damn. "You know I don't like to be called Mr. Ketchum, but here you are again, calling me that."

"Gee, I'm sorry." He didn't look sorry, though, he looked angry. I couldn't blame him.

37

"And I'm very tired of your generalized butt-kissing, Tommy. I really am. Everybody up here believes that you're a hard worker and a good kid. No need to keep reminding us. Your work speaks for itself."

In the silence that followed I realized that I'd hurt his feelings and managed to make myself feel very foolish in the process.

"Gee, I—"

Thank God there was a knock on the door just then and thank God it was Clay Traynor and thank God he did his usual boorish number and came right in without me inviting him.

Except when I got a better look at him I saw he was not wearing his standard smirk. The eyes looked bad and a tiny, deadly twitch could be seen on the right edge of his mouth.

He looked like he couldn't decide whether to ask me for some fatherly advice or to smash my face in.

He glanced at Tommy as if the kid were one of life's real annoyances, then dropped himself into one of the chairs across from my desk.

I nodded to Tommy. "We'll talk more later."

By now Tommy was white. The poor bastard probably thought he was on the verge of being fired.

"It's OK, Tommy," I said. "Everything's OK."

"You sure?" he said.

"Yeah, I'm sure."

He scanned my face for any trace of insincerity. Finding none seemed to relax him.

"OK," he said, "later."

After Tommy had closed the door behind him, Clay said, "You like that kid?"

I shrugged. "He's all right. Just tries a little too hard sometimes."

"Something about him . . ." He sighed and stared into the fists that sat in his lap. The way his head wagged, the way his eyes weren't quite in focus, I could see that he was drunk from both the night before and from whatever he'd needed to get himself going this morning. He had shaved but there were too many nicks and he had washed his hair but there was too much grease on it and he had changed clothes but the red tie was too sporty for the button-down shirt. "Poor sonofabitch," he said. Obviously he was through talking about Tommy. He was talking about Denny. "Goddamn good guy . . ." he said and tears started in his eyes and the twitch on the side of his mouth got much, much worse. "Goddamn good buddy of mine . . ."

I let him find his own pace for expressing the things he needed to say.

"Who the hell coulda done it?" he said after a time.

"I don't know."

He smiled a worn smile. "Probably some husband whose old lady he was poking."

"Could be."

"The poor sonofabitch," he said.

"Yeah."

"I mean, I know you two didn't get along especially well. But he admired your talents, Michael. He really did."

"Well, for what it's worth, I admired his."

Much as Tommy had done, he searched my face for any evidence of insincerity. Then he went back into his semistupor.

I got up and went over to the dry bar and made him the kind of drink sailors dream of three months out to sea. He didn't even look up, just took it automatically and began drinking immediately.

Five minutes later, the booze wrought something like a miracle. The twitch stopped. His eye grew bright. He sat up straighter in the chair.

"It could have been robbery," he said. The hopeful tone of his voice surprised me—as if he were going to wish robbery into being the motive.

I had never seen Clay seem so young or vulnerable. Maybe it was weakness from his hangover. Whatever, his almost clinging presence bothered me.

"Robbery seems pretty unlikely, Clay," I said. "From what the cop said, I mean. All those stab wounds."

"Some robbers are junkies. They can get crazy—"

I shook my head. "I don't think so."

Clay pulled himself to the edge of the chair.

"I suppose you're wondering about the account," he said.

I shrugged. "I guess right now I'm more wondering about Denny."

Some of the old fire caught in his face. "You didn't like him. Why the hell pretend otherwise?"

His anger gave the room a heat in the overcast day. "He was still my partner and had been for twelve years."

He calmed down. "I just wanted to assure you that if I have anything to do with it, the account will be staying here."

Now, since most advertising people are certified paranoids, the most significant words in his statement were not the reassurance that the account would be staying here—but rather the phrase "if I have anything to do with it."

In that little phrase was an obscure and ominous meaning that made me forget all about Denny and made me think instead of losing half my business—at a minimum. And failing all the people depending on me.

The catch was . . . Clay, being a vainglorious bastard, could never admit that his cousin Ron had any real influence on his decisions.

Why would he admit that Ron actually called most of the shots now?

"I mean," Clay said, "I guess you know all about Ron's friend Bill Spencer."

Yeah, I knew all about Ron's friend Bill Spencer. Spence was president of the largest agency in the city and our chief rival. Spence and Ron were golfing buddies. Ron had every intention of someday driving a wedge between Clay and my agency—whatever it took. Then Spence would have the account.

"Hey," Clay laughed, "no need to look all shook up. I just mentioned that to let you know that I'd like to keep right on working with you."

The way I sighed—relief—was embarrassing. To me, anyway. Clay laughed again. He found me amusing.

"Of course," he said, "I'm going to have to ask you certain favors from time to time."

"Hell, yes," I said. I would rather have talked about the quality of work he was getting from Harris-Ketchum—which was damned good; sales were up and our stuff consistently won awards—but if he wanted to talk about favors, sure, fine, all right. That's what I was here for.

"Any time," I said, having visions of spending long nights with him at any number of sleazy watering holes, or hiking through the woods in order to beat the shit out of defenseless little animals.

Favors. He'd come to the right place. No doubt about that.

"Well then," he said, "how about starting right now?"

"Sure. What can I do for you?"

"Well," he said, studying his Stetson, "Denny has something of mine that I'd really like back."

"I'll help you find it. No problem, Clay."

He glanced at me. I hadn't ever seen him sweat before. His face was slick. "Now that he's dead, the thing he had doesn't mean anything. What I need now is another kind of favor."

"Absolutely."

"See, last night I decided to run by his place and pick up this thing . . ." He glanced furtively around the office—

Tommy had had the good sense to close the door behind him. " . . . I found him there. Already dead."

"Jesus."

He leaned closer. Now we were co-conspirators. "You can imagine I don't want to be implicated in any way . . ." He looked at me significantly. "That would give Ron all the ammunition he needs to take over the presidency of Traynor . . ." He smiled nervously. "The Board of Directors— well, you know what they think of me already. If I were implicated—well, both you and I would be out of a job."

"This favor you need—" I started to say.

"What I need," he said, "I guess you'd call it an alibi."

Which was just when Detective Bonnell chose to knock on the door.

SEVEN

"Damn," Clay Traynor said after Bonnell had identified himself from behind the closed door.

I shot him a wary glance, then got up, walked around my desk, and opened the door.

"Hope I'm not disturbing you," Bonnell said. He was a large man who could have been mistaken for fat until you noticed how tightly his flesh clung to his facial bones. Obviously he took care of himself. He wore a brown suit and tan topcoat without looking quite comfortable in either. He appeared to be in his early fifties, yet he had retained an animal energy that said he'd rather be working on the docks somewhere, or putting up a house. His dark, intelligent eyes held irony and made him seem all the more dangerous.

Now I had to lie not only about myself last night—about Mr. and Mrs. Traynor as well. Even in death, Denny kept my life stirred up.

"You mind?" Bonnell said, showing his cigarette pack as if he were on a commercial. I hadn't seen Chesterfields since my college days, especially the stubby ones. I associated them with Humphrey Bogart—that was the brand he'd been rumored to smoke, right up till his death from lung cancer.

Bonnell took the chair opposite Clay's. After he lit up, he

took a small notebook from his topcoat pocket, flicked a ball-point into action, and said, "I've been talking to several people here about Mr. Harris. Seems to be some difference of opinion about him."

I shrugged. "I'm sure that's true."

The dark eyes narrowed. "We didn't get much of a chance to talk earlier, Mr. Ketchum. I guess I didn't get any real understanding of how you felt about him."

"He was my partner."

He smiled, looked over to Clay. "Mr. Ketchum here is a very cautious man."

Clay smiled nervously in return. Hard to believe that a spoiled adolescent like Clay could ever have his faith shaken in the power of his old man's money—but there it was. He looked miserable and guilty and ready to fly apart. "Yeah, he is kinda cautious, I guess."

Bonnell kept his eyes on him long enough that Clay started squirming in the chair.

By now I had half convicted Clay in my mind. Somehow he'd found out about Cindy's affair with Denny. Somehow he'd gone to Denny's and . . .

. . .and here I was about to provide him with an alibi. He hadn't been kidding about the Board of Directors. He held their confidence only by a slim margin. Any kind of scandal would lose that margin. And then the account would absolutely change agencies . . .

"How about it?" Bonnell pressed. "How did you feel about your partner?"

I decided to be diplomatic without exactly lying. After talking to various people who worked at the agency, Bonnell would be well aware of the strained relationship between Denny and me. I knew, for example, that he'd talked to Gettig, the producer I'd argued with yesterday about Denny's authority to make final decisions on commercials—Gettig was my enemy. He would be delighted to see me come under

44

suspicion. As would Wickes in accounting—not to mention his secretary, Belinda Matson . . .

"We had our differences, I suppose."

"You suppose?" The irony was in his voice as well as his eyes.

"Are you accusing me of something?"

He smiled. "Not that I know of."

Then he turned to Clay. "My impression of you and Mr. Harris is that you were good friends, is that right?"

Clay couldn't find his voice. He had to clear his throat a few times before he could speak.

I had a vision of him plunging a knife into Denny's back again and again in a sexual rage over his unfaithful wife . . .

"Very good friends," he said, almost voiceless.

Bonnell studied him. "You have a cold, Mr. Traynor? I guess thcy're going around."

"Yeah. Cold," Clay said. What an actor.

By now Bonnell's method was clear. He had spoken briefly to Clay and me, gotten suspicious about something we'd said or done, then gone through the rest of the agency to corroborate his impression. By the time he got back to us, he'd convinced himself that one of us was the perfect candidate for the state's recently reinstated electric chair.

"Did you see Denny yesterday?" Bonnell asked me. Before I could answer, he stubbed out his cigarette with two nicotine-yellowed fingers. I could imagine what his lungs looked like . . .

"No," I said. As I said it I realized how quickly I'd spoken. Too quickly.

He wrote something in his notebook. He did it with great flourish, flicking his wrist before he began.

"How about you Mr. Traynor?"

Clay did his usual bad job of covering for himself. Before he spoke he looked at me—as if for guidance. Then he turned back to Bonnell. "Uh-uh. I didn't see him, either."

If there was ever a time for Clay to be his usual arrogant, swaggering self, it was now. Instead he'd become a shrinking violet. All that inflated macho crap—gone.

Bonnell watched both of us, the irony back. "So neither of you men saw him?"

"No," I said.

"No," Clay said.

"Who do you think would have reason to kill him?" Bonnell said.

"Personally, from what you said," Clay said, "it sounds like robbery to me."

"Not to me, Mr. Traynor," Bonnell said. "I feel sure this was done by somebody who knew him and knew him well."

"Act of passion?" I said.

"Precisely." He lit another Chesterfield. The sulphur smell from the match stayed on the air a long moment, not unpleasantly. "Maybe what we're talking about here is a jealous husband—or jealous lover at any rate." A kind of chuckle came into his throat. I qualify that only because the noise he made was far more ominous than a chuckle. "From every person I talked to, I got the impression that Mr. Harris was not a stranger to love affairs, particularly with other men's wives."

As he spoke he focused on me, not on Clay.

Now it was my turn to clear my voice, to reach far down the well of my throat and try to dredge up some words. "I didn't think people got that bent out of shape anymore. I mean, these are supposedly liberated times."

"Not that liberated, I'm afraid, Mr. Ketchum." The melancholy in his voice seemed genuine, the irony gone from his gaze. For that instant I wondered if Clay and I weren't being paranoid. Maybe because we had things to hide we were overinterpreting everything Bonnell said. Maybe he didn't suspect us at all . . .

"I guess I'm still a little unclear," Bonnell said, "about

how you and Denny Harris met each other." He had his pen poised. "Maybe you could run through that for me. Maybe that will help me get a better picture of Mr. Harris."

Though I wasn't sure why he wanted to know—though I was starting to get suspicious again—I ran through it for him, the same story I'd gone through myself many times.

I had met Denny Harris when he was an assistant account exec at a large agency where I was a junior copywriter. We shared a hard-core ambition for success. At the large agency we wound up in control of our own team, attracting the second-largest account the agency had, and winning a dozen or so national awards for our work on two or three accounts. Inevitably, we started talking about having our own agency. My wife was equally ambitious. She thought it was a great idea. And that's how it came about. We had opened shop ten years before in a crackerbox over by the river. We did well enough that we had moved downtown before a year was over. Except our relationship started falling apart. Denny had always been the troublesome little boy. He'd managed to be fetching about it—for a while. But I got sick of the hangovers, of the black eyes he occasionally sported, of the innumerable female employees who moped around the shop after he had visited them vampirelike the night before.

I also began to wonder about the finances of our shop. I was creative director and in charge of all writing, art, and production. Denny was to be in charge of business. But he began being secretive about things. His expense account, for example, swelled beyond recognition. I began to wonder if he ever paid for anything himself. Conservative by nature, I tended to leave everything I could in the business. I asked Wickes about what was going on many times—and many times he responded the same way, by showing me financial statements I didn't quite understand, no matter how hard I tried.

Along with the perilous business situation, my marriage

began to suffer, (which, of course, I didn't share with Bonnell). It was obvious to everybody but me apparently that my wife Sylvia and I had nothing in common anymore. She had taken up the bar scene—the leper colony I referred to earlier—abdicating, as I saw it, her responsibilities as both wife and mother. Fortunately, our kids were old enough that they could accept the inevitable. They accepted it with much more grace than I did. Particularly after she told me she had had lovers over the past three years . . .

"I know how all this sounds," I said to Bonnell. "I wish I could say I liked Denny—I'd feel better about myself if I could—but I didn't." I shook my head. "But I didn't kill him, either."

"I have to ask you something . . ." Bonnell began.

And then I knew that Sarah had told him. She was the only person up here who knew it—Denny had told her one day ostensibly because he felt guilty about it and needed to unburden himself; what he was really trying to do was establish himself forever as the dominant figure on this particular landscape. I didn't blame her, not really. She was being a good citizen, that was all, trying to help the police do their job the best way possible.

"Your wife—" Bonnell began.

"—Ex-wife—"

"—had a brief affair with Denny Harris. Is that right?"

I nodded.

I could see by the indifferent way Clay looked that he'd known already. So much for shocking revelations. I suppose Denny had told everybody. I saw a terrible kind of justice in it—the lepers that Sylvia saw as so glittering and so much fun, using her for nothing more than cocktail chatter and gossip.

"You were married while this was going on?" Bonnell asked.

48

"Yes, though I didn't know about it until after I'd filed for divorce."

"You didn't end your business relationship?"

I shrugged. "By then it didn't matter. I was pretty much numb."

Bonnell nodded. "Yeah, I went through a divorce myself. I know what you mean." Human—at last, and however briefly.

"I didn't kill him. I really didn't," I said.

He assessed me. He seemed to believe me—or was I just hoping?

"I'm going to have to ask both you gentlemen where you were last evening. We don't have a medical examiner's report yet, but the lab is estimating the death at late afternoon—say around six o'clock."

Which was when Clay Traynor said, in the cocky way I was used to, "Hate to spoil your fun, Bonnell. But we were together, weren't we Michael? Working late right here in this office." The hangdog Clay and the arrogant one.

The irony returned to Bonnell's gaze. He looked at me. "True, Mr. Ketchum?"

At first I couldn't get it out—the single syllable that would make me a perjurer.

"Mr. Ketchum?" Bonnell repeated.

I looked at Clay, who was stupidly smiling. I thought of my kids and my old man in the nursing home, his paperlike flesh. The eyes that did not quite know me when I bent to kiss him. Losing the agency would cut me adrift—I wouldn't be able to help them.

"Yes," I said. "True."

EIGHT

Around noon I decided to close the office for the rest of the day. Not out of any respect for Denny, of course—though I was beginning to feel guilty that my thoughts weren't at least occasionally reverent—but rather because nobody was getting anything done.

Clay Traynor had left a few minutes after Bonnell. Traynor had been grinning as he exited. Apparently he wasn't feeling any worse about his good friend Denny than I was.

I closed my door and stood at the window looking down on the city. The sky was the slate gray it had been the past few days. Without snow to accompany them, the Christmas decorations hanging everywhere looked more hopeful than real—like the decorations you see in balmy Florida around the holidays. Shoppers leaned into the bitter wind and fled into storefronts for respite. Even shopping was edged with travail these days—at least that's how I'd come to see the world.

A knock on my door—discreet as only Sarah Anders could make it—caused me to turn around and get it over with. Sarah was going to apologize and I was going to accept—sincerely—and that was going to be that.

When I let her in, her eyes were red from crying and her

voice was hoarse. She daubed at her cheeks with a handkerchief that had seen extra duty in the past few hours. "I can't believe it," she said. "Dead."

I guided her to a chair.

I went back behind my desk and sat down and let her sniffle and sob until she was done.

Finally, she looked up and said, "I have to tell you something, Michael."

I stared across at her, trying to look as pleasant as possible. "I know what you're going to tell me, Sarah."

"You do?"

I nodded. "That you had to tell Detective Bonnell that Denny and my ex-wife had a small affair."

She put her head down, stared at her lap, at her fingers knotted around her handkerchief. "I'm sorry."

"I understand."

"Really?"

"Yeah. Really, Sarah."

"I was afraid you'd . . . ." She shook her head, started crying again. " . . .afraid you'd hate me."

I can't tell you why, but watching her just then I was struck by a false note. Maybe it was the way she started and stopped crying with such regularity. Maybe it was the curious lack of conviction in her apology. Whatever, I was aware that I was watching a performance rather than anything spontaneous—but I couldn't pinpoint why.

Which led me to wonder for the first time—letting my anger and suspicions come out—why she'd "had to" tell Bonnell about Denny and my ex-wife at all. Had he come right out and asked her if she suspected that I was the killer? Damned unlikely. How had the subject come up unless she'd brought it up herself?

"Why don't you go home, Sarah," I said, as kindly as possible.

She glanced up. Started sniffling again. She was a bad actress.

Looking at her, I realized I was in the throes of a kind of madness. I didn't trust Sarah, Clay Traynor, Cindy Traynor, Bonnell, or Merle or Julie Wickes—and I saw all of them as knowing far more than they were letting on. I needed to turn to somebody, talk to somebody—but who? When you get that sense of isolation, that sense that you can confide in no one, then you're easing open the door of madness and peering inside.

Sarah stood up.

"I just can't imagine who'd do anything like this," she said. "He . . . he had his faults but . . ."

That was the only genuine-sounding thing she'd said since coming in here. Even when he was dead, she wanted to mother and protect him. Maybe in a curious way I felt jealous—that she'd never expressed any protective feelings toward me. Apparently I wasn't the kind of guy women enjoy mothering.

I walked her to the door. She kissed me on the cheek with her warm, wet face, then clutched my hand. It was the kind of thing you expected at graveside, very dramatic rather than low-key and earnest.

Then she turned back and stared at me a moment. "I know you may not believe this, but deep down, he really respected you. I know he did."

Sure he did, Sarah. About as much as I respected Hitler.

I spent the next few hours going over the work load that lay ahead for the next few weeks. If I needed any reminder of how critical the Traynor account was to the preservation of Harris-Ketchum, this was it.

Two television and six radio spots and four print ads needed to be produced for the Traynor account, along with forty-two different pieces of collateral, meaning brochures, catalog pages, point-of-purchase cards, etc. Much of the work would yield us fifteen percent for placing it in various mediums, all of which amounted to several hundred thousand dollars, and this for a very small campaign. In the parlance of the trade, Traynor was a "cash cow," meaning it could be milked for our sustenance.

And—if we were to meet overhead—it needed to be milked for every possible penny.

Not noble, perhaps, but true.

Around three, with a headache starting to work through my frontal lobes, I decided to walk through the shop, kind of an inspection now that I would be running the place myself. I wasn't sure what provisions Denny had made in his will for his part of the agency, but I felt sure he would have left it to somebody outside the business.

Ordinarily, I didn't like walking the length and breadth of the shop because it was too much like spying: Douglas MacArthur inspecting all the funny little yellow troops at his command. Today, though, alone, I picked up layouts, looked at copy, played some videotapes, and in general learned that we could turn out good creative work on a rather consistent basis.

I was headed back toward my office after spending an hour in the shop when I heard the noise coming from Denny's office.

At first I thought it might be Bonnell back again, but there was a furtive edge to the sounds of drawers being opened and closed, closets being searched . . .

On impulse, I picked up a knife used for cutting packing tape as I moved closer to Denny's office . . .

They were so busy they didn't even hear me. Both of them looked sweaty, almost feverish, they were working so quickly.

"Hello," I said.

Sarah Anders looked up first. Her tears were long gone, replaced now with a resolute kind of anger.

Then Gettig whirled to look at me. He had been working on the wall safe Denny kept behind the framed photograph of his father, while Sarah had been working through the bookcase, dropping books as she went.

As usual, Gettig was dressed like the lead in a beer commercial. Today he was trying to look like a Jack London seaman—thick black turtleneck, heavy belt holding up designer jeans. I almost expected him to call me "matey." Instead, he said, "Get the hell out of here." Then he started stalking toward me.

I'm not going to pretend that I'm tough, or even especially physically adept. But at that precise moment I had two things going for me. One, I was composed enough that I could set my balance; two, I genuinely disliked Gettig, which made what I was about to do a very pleasant task.

I got him a good clean shot across the jaw and he sagged before I could get him with another one. He slumped against the desk, his eyes vague.

Sarah grabbed my arm. "Don't hit him again, Michael. Please."

It was in her voice and gaze, something I wouldn't have ever suspected. I wondered how and when they'd gotten together—and why. I couldn't imagine an intelligent, sensitive woman like Sarah with a cartoon like Gettig. But there it was—pity and fear and passion in her eyes and voice all at the same time.

"What are you looking for Sarah?" I snapped.

"Just . . ." She seemed on the verge of talking when Gettig regained his feet.

"Don't tell him a damned thing!" he said.

Sarah flushed. "Ron, please . . ."

I thought of Sarah's plump, friendly husband sitting out in

54

the suburbs somewhere. Well, I supposed that for all his flaws, Gettig was exciting in his foolish way . . .

"Get out," I said. Obviously neither of them was going to talk.

"He's got something of mine," Gettig said, rubbing his jaw. "I want it."

"Take it up with his estate."

Sarah, sensing that the punches were going to start flying again, took Gettig's arm. He wrenched it away violently. She looked as if God had just spurned her.

Then Gettig said, "C'mon," and stormed out.

She stared at me then followed him out, turning back only at the last. "Denny really did have something that belonged to Ron."

I thought of Clay Traynor using similar words to explain why he'd gone out to Denny's last night.

"Sarah, why the hell would you get mixed up with somebody like Gettig?"

Anger flashed across her eyes. "You don't have a right to judge me!"

Her words hurt me just enough—obviously I did have a tendency to be overly judgmental—that I could do nothing but shake my head.

Then she followed her lover out and disappeared down the hall.

For the next ten minutes the echoes of all the anger rang in the room. I sat in Denny's desk chair and thought of the better times when we'd been younger and gotten along. I looked at the awards that covered one entire wall and thought of all the great work we'd done over the years, despite any number of personal ups and downs.

It was while I was mellowing out that I started wondering again what it was that Gettig and Sarah had been looking for. On the floor around my feet were small piles of stuff they'd left from their search. I started putting the things back into the drawers they'd been taken from.

Which was when I found the newspaper clipping about the robbery.

At the time it didn't make the least bit of sense to me and I wondered why Denny had kept it in his desk at all.

I also wondered why I felt compelled to put the clipping in my pocket and take it along with mc when I went home.

NINE

By the time I reached the parking garage, a winter dusk had settled over the chill air. The garage was in shadows. On my way to my car I heard my name called out cheerfully. Ahead of me in the gloom, I saw Tommy Byrnes wave and walk toward me.

My stomach did unpleasant things. We hadn't really talked since our conversation in my office. I was going to have to be very nice and very apologetic and at the moment the prospect of being either wearied me.

Tommy came toward me like a shy animal. "Hi," he said.

I nodded. Decided to get it over with quickly. "Sorry about yesterday, Tommy. I'm not in the best frame of mind. You know how that goes—little things, insignificant things, irritate me. I want you to know I think you're doing a good job."

"Thanks," he said. Obviously he was half afraid to speak, afraid he'd make me angry again.

We walked to our cars in tense silence.

"I really do want to be in advertising," he said finally.

"I know you do, Tommy. I just can't figure out why."

He was surprised. "But it's a great field, Michael." He was still self-conscious about calling me by my first name but he was learning. "I mean, it's really creative."

"I don't think so," I said.

"You don't? Really?"

"We're dabblers, Tommy. That's what most of us are. We can't write novels or poetry so we dabble at writing copy and make a very big thing of how 'creative' we are. Or we can't paint seriously so we go on about how inventive we are and throw a lot of awards dinners so that everybody will know that we're important. In a way, the account executives are the most honest of all of us. They're whores and most of them don't pretend to be anything else." I looked over at his young, shocked face. This wasn't anything remotely resembling what his professors would be telling him—particularly not with the venom I could hear in my voice.

"So how come you stay in it, then?"

"Very simple. There's nothing else I can do that people will pay me half as well for."

"But you're a good writer. You really are."

This time I could sense he wasn't offering idle ass-kissing. He was being sincere.

"A good copywriter, Tommy. You've got to make that distinction. It's one thing to write a clever little ad and it's another thing entirely to write something worthwhile."

"But you've won Clios. That should be worth something."

"It wouldn't be worth a hell of a lot to Hemingway." I laughed. "Tommy, this is a field where agency people who help pollute the air and feed chemicals into the food supply are given statues of appreciation." I stopped at my car and clapped him on the shoulder. "There I go again, Tommy. Sorry. I'm not in the best of moods."

"I still want to be in advertising." He had received the True Calling and his voice trembled with it now. Despite my cynicism he preferred to believe that advertising was just as important and glamorous and soul-sustaining as his advertising professor told him it was. "Well, at least I'm glad you're not still mad at me," he added.

58

I nodded and waved goodnight and watched him walk into the shadows at the far end of the ramp.

Then I opened the door to my own car. The overhead light came on. In the dimness I saw Cindy Traynor.

All she said was, "God, I'm freezing to death. Hurry up. Please."

TEN

She didn't seem aware when I got in and closed the door. She just stared straight ahead. Obviously she was looking at much more than the rough concrete wall.

"Are you all right?" I asked.

Nothing.

"You must be freezing, Cindy."

Nothing.

I turned on the heater. Played the radio. Sat back and lit a cigarette.

"I'm sorry about having you followed," I said.

"I know." Her voice, ethereal, was nonetheless startling in the quiet.

I decided to start over again. Gently. "How long have you been here?" Her car was parked next to mine.

"An hour. I'm not sure."

I reached over and touched the tip of her nose. It felt like a piece of ice. I smiled. "At least an hour."

"I talked to the young kid for a while."

I looked at Tommy Byrnes's retreating car. "Tommy?"

"Yes. He saw me sitting here and came over. He's very nice."

My eyes studied her in the darkness, her blondness, the

60

slightly drugged beauty of her features. She looked tired. She sighed, tried something like a smile. "I don't know why I came here."

"To talk, I suppose. I need to talk to somebody, too. Given the circumstances, I'd say that's pretty normal."

"This afternoon I had some wine and took a Librium, and I thought they would help me sleep but they haven't." She shrugged. "I've never been involved in anything like this, have you?"

"No."

"My parents were very strict Lutherans. Very strict. They didn't prepare me to commit adultery or be involved in murder cases." The muzziness of her voice was starting to have a sexual effect on me, like the slow blue gaze of her sleepy eyes. "Do you ever think about death?"

"You know what?" I said. "Maybe there's a better place to have a discussion like this one."

"You didn't answer my question."

"Sure, I think about death."

"Does it scare you?"

"Yes."

"Do you believe in God?"

"Sort of."

"Yeah, me too. Sort of. My mother believes in Him absolutely and that's a great comfort to her. Last Thanksgiving I walked in on her. She was on her hands and knees, praying. I was really moved. I wish I could be like that but I'm afraid I lead a different kind of life, don't I?"

I laughed. "Maybe it's our generation."

She laughed too. "That's a handy excuse, anyway." She paused. "I was going to go into the agency and get you but I was afraid I'd run into Clay."

"He left a few hours ago."

"He's afraid."

"I know."

"I feel sorry for him. He doesn't know what to do."

I hesitated. "You know, there's a possibility he may have killed Denny."

She shook her head. "There's a possibility that any number of us may have killed Denny." She folded her hands primly and went back to staring at the wall. Then, "Where did you have in mind to go?"

"To my apartment."

"Maybe you've got the wrong impression of me. I really don't sleep around. Sorry. Denny's the only affair I ever had."

"I thought maybe we could talk."

"We're talking here."

"Where we could be more comfortable, I mean."

"I'm very vulnerable right now. I might say yes to something I'd regret."

"Did you kill him?"

"No. Did you?"

"No."

"Do you think my husband did?"

"I don't know," I said.

"Is your apartment nice?"

"It's tolerable."

"Does it have a fireplace?"

"Yes."

"Please don't try to get me into bed, all right?"

"All right."

"Promise?"

"Yes. Promise."

"The first time I ever met Clay he was in the college library studying a Shakespeare play. He was very nice-looking and very clean-cut and he had this little-boy look of confusion on his face whenever he came to a part that he didn't understand. He sort of fascinated me—just watching him, I mean—because I sensed that here was somebody I could help. I usually attracted the type of men who ruled the earth, if you know what I mean. Everything I wanted to do was silly; I was supposed to just listen to them and everything would be fine.

"But Clay really needed somebody. He put on the swagger act but he was really lost. For one thing he was completely overshadowed by his father, who'd built the Traynor company from nothing. Both Clay and his father knew that Clay could never run the company. That's why Clay's father started grooming his nephew to take over the reins—even though Clay would always be called president—when the nephew was only fifteen years old. Clay told me that his cousin spent half his Saturdays at the company with Clay's father. Clay was never invited and he didn't seem to care. He was into his pleasures."

She was curled up at the opposite end of the couch from me. For the past three hours we'd found a respite from the events pressing in on us. I'd found some decent frozen food to pop into the microwave; we'd watched the fog curl around the window in my front room, and the fire crackled in the shadows. I was starting to trust her and like her and in the lazy moments of our time here, I sensed she was experiencing the same thing. She was not the woman I'd stereotyped her into being, particularly as she talked about Clay and how much she'd loved him once and how the loss of their love had crushed her. I knew what she was talking about.

"The one thing people never give Clay as president is that he was very good as a representative of the company at one time. Until he got so caught up with all his women." She paused, touching her head as if she had a migraine. "I thought maybe his fascination for other women would pass— I even used to pray about it—but it never did. And all the while he was getting worse and worse at his job. That's when his cousin really started accumulating power.

"Anyway, I suppose that's why I had hope for us for so long despite a lot of evidence to the contrary." She smiled with a melancholy that revitalized her face. "You know, I always tried to believe that he was just as blameless as he said he was—that all the nights he was gone he was just innocently playing poker or having a few drinks with his buddies. This was back in the sixties, the early sixties, you understand, when it was still possible to delude yourself that way." She laughed gently, sadly. "Then one night at a party I went out to our car and I found him in the back seat with a young girl. They were both naked. The human body had never disgusted me before—but it did then. It was two years before I'd even look at myself in the mirror. I just kept thinking of them in the back seat. I admit it probably wasn't easy for Clay during that time. I could have forgiven him and we could have taken up our lives again. I don't know how many times I tried—hoped.

"We didn't make love for two years. His father would have disinherited him if we divorced, so we had to keep up pretenses. Clay had his life and I had mine—which mostly consisted of watching TV and taking tranquilizers and seeing shrinks. It never occurred to me to take a lover, even during the seventies when all my female friends had lovers all the time. The only reason I finally went to bed with Denny was because I found out about Clay and the girl in your accounting department. What's her name—Belinda?"

"Belinda Matson?" The name rocked me. Literally. I straightened up, my drowsiness gone.

"You sound surprised?"

I laughed. Bitterly. "What a snake pit it all is."

"Well, that's the only reason I went to bed with Denny. One night I was downtown and I saw Clay and this Belinda. I recognized her from your agency party. I'd thought by that time that I was beyond caring, but it hurt me. Well, I ran into Denny an hour later and he bought me a drink and . . ." She shook her head. "We were both very drunk. I have doubts that he even remembered it exactly. The odd thing was, I never enjoyed it—never cared about him one way or the other. It was crazy. I just needed to be with somebody, even somebody like him."

But I was still thinking of Belinda Matson and Clay—and of poor slob Merle Wickes, who probably thought he was Belinda's only lover.

She stared into the fire. "I wrote him the note you found because I was trying to make myself feel a little better about committing adultery. I thought maybe if I could convince myself that I actually cared for Denny . . . My mother produced a much better Lutheran than she realized. I was going to cut it off with Denny, which is why I'd gone to his place last night. But . . ."

She surprised me by leaning over and taking my hands in hers. "I have to tell you something, but I'm afraid."

I shook my head. "I guess we don't have any choice except to trust each other now."

"I'm afraid for Clay."

"Why?"

"Because . . ." She paused. "When I pulled up in Denny's driveway last night, I saw Clay's car there. I think he overheard Denny and me talking on the phone one night. Anyway I panicked and backed out and parked down the road. Then I saw Clay come running out. He didn't see me, he was too wild to see anything." She shuddered. "I think Clay killed him."

"I'm his alibi otherwise."

"What?"

I told her about the lie I'd told Detective Bonnell to clear Clay.

"So you're not going to help the police and neither am I," she said.

"Maybe he didn't do it."

"Do you believe that?"

"I don't know what to believe."

And then I kissed her.

It happened that suddenly and inevitably. I eased her back against the couch and what I'd intended for a chaste kiss of friendship became something I could hardly control. I felt the flesh of her beneath and against me, the taste of her mouth and the scent of her hair and the tang of her skin.

"Please," she said, pushing away, "you promised."

All I could do was sit there, jangled as I'd been after finding Denny, lost in my desires and terrors.

She moved quickly, to the closet where I'd put her coat, and then to the front door.

I started to stand up but she put up a stopping hand.

She looked weary again. Confused. "I'm starting to feel as sorry for us as I do for Clay," she said.

She shook her lovely head and was gone.

ELEVEN

The call came—according to the digital clock next to my bed—at 2:28 A.M.

By the time I'd reached bed I'd been exhausted enough to sleep till noon.

Responding to the call was not easy. I had to swim upward through several miles of subconsciousness and then groggily figure out where the phone was and how to operate it.

He might have been selling insurance, the way he sounded so chipper and bright. A deal I couldn't refuse.

"Mr. Ketchum," he boomed.

"Huh, wha—"

"Mr. Ketchum, I realize it's late—or early—depending on your point of view—but I have got to talk to you about something that both of us have a mutual interest in."

And then I realized who I was talking to. The queer bird with the Coke-bottle glasses and the pale flesh and the sinister black clothing.

Stokes. The private detective I'd hired.

"I'd like to come over, Mr. Ketchum."

"Now?" I said, startled.

"If you wouldn't mind."

"God. Can't it wait until morning?"

"By morning, Mr. Ketchum, you could very well be out of business."

"Damn," I said.

"Twenty minutes," he said.

And hung up.

Coffee, cigarettes, soaking my face in cold water, and a terrible certainty that Stokes wasn't kidding about his bad news brought me awake in less than fifteen minutes.

Because patience is not among my chief virtues anyway, the remaining twenty-minute wait caused me to get a workout by pacing the living room. I was eager to ask him what Merle Wickes had been doing at his office.

I was glancing out the window when I saw headlights wash against the naked trees running along the edge of the parking area.

Then it was another few—but interminable—minutes before I heard steps trudging up the stairs. Stokes had a knock like somebody throwing an anvil against a piece of fiberboard. I half expected to see the door sag in the middle under the pressure of his fist.

When I opened the door and saw him, I wondered for the first time if Stokes ever changed clothes. His attire contributed to both sinister and comic impressions. He wore the double-knit black sport coat with lapels wide enough to play shuffleboard on. His tie was one of those striped jobs that men used to affect with leisure suits—except his stripes ran to the funereal—a gray stripe, then a black stripe, then a gray stripe. Real festive stuff—as Stokes was festive. The doughy face was half-covered by huge eyeglasses thick as the bottoms of drinking glasses. Behind them swam two eyes that seemed to be half blind, squinting. The rest of his face was pinched—a sharp, disapproving nose; a thin, disapproving mouth—sitting on top of a pear-shaped body that, like his face, managed to convey the sinister and the comic.

68

As he came in, he said, looking around, "Shoulda figured you'd have money, Ketchum."

Which told me a lot about Mr. Stokes. If he thought I had money—the furniture was mostly from secondhand stores, literally—then he must really be from hunger. Maybe he was responding to the decor, which had been done free of charge by a onetime girlfriend of mine. But whatever his reason for saying it, he made the remark unpleasant, full of envy and even menace.

"You want a drink?" I said. I didn't sound any happier about seeing him than he'd sounded about seeing me.

"Just a minute," he said, waving me off.

He stood in the middle of my living room, smelling like a wet dog.

"People's places," he said, almost to himself, "they tell you secrets sometimes. All you have to do is stand still and look them over."

Stokes was one of those people who give other people the creeps—though you might not exactly be able to say why. You wouldn't be surprised to see his photo on the tube in conjunction with the ax deaths of a suburban couple and their children. I'd picked a honey when I'd called Federated Investigation Services. He'd been smart enough—each of us has some advertising instincts—to pick the Federated name, which gave him a lot more weight in the Yellow Pages than A-1 or Nocturne, which is way too dramatic. Federated sounds vaguely like a bank. I'd expected somebody in pinstripes with a college degree who just happened to carry a Mauser. Instead, I got Stokes here.

"You learn all my secrets yet?" I said, more harshly than I'd intended.

A smirk parted his lips, revealing teeth the color of a urine specimen. I had hoped he would take the money I paid him and go straight to his dentist's. "You'd be surprised what I know," he said.

To hell with him. I went over and fixed myself another drink. Meanwhile, he kept looking around my apartment.

As I was coming around the tiny wet bar, I saw the newspaper clipping I'd taken from my suitcoat earlier. The one about the robbery I'd found in Denny Harris's desk. I studied it a moment, then decided to leave it where it was. I had no intention of sharing it with Stokes. I'd already decided to pay him off and get rid of him.

He lit a Camel from a crumpled pack, a real Camel, not one of those sissified things they push these days. No wonder his teeth looked the way they did.

I went over to the couch and sat on the edge while Stokes finished examining a Chagall lithograph I own, my only expensive indulgence since the divorce.

When he finished, he turned around and said, "Guess where I was last night."

"Your mom's?" I joked.

For the first time since I'd met him, he showed anger. He pushed his body forward. His eyes flashed. "I don't make jokes about my mother." He had to somewhere near fifty. That he was that sensitive about his mother made me very suspicious, made him all the more odd and dangerous in my mind.

"Sorry," I said, "if I offended you." I could not quite get the irony out of my voice, a problem I sometimes have.

I decided not to let him rest. He'd been no help to me. I'd left my card last night and he hadn't called back. I wanted him off the case and out of my life.

"I want you to submit your bill," I said.

A kind of smirk touched his mouth. "You firing me?"

"You could call it that."

He looked around again. "Guy lives in a place like this, he gets the idea he can do anything he wants, push anybody around, I guess."

"Yeah," I said, "that's me OK. A regular Mussolini."

70

He faced me. "You know something, Ketchum?"

"What?"

"You're a punk."

"Gee, thanks."

"You got a fancy apartment, fancy business, you think you know everything. You don't know shit."

"That's been pointed out to me. Many times."

"Well, it's true."

"So you've told me."

He reached inside his coat and pulled out a manila envelope. "I'm gonna have you do me a little favor," he said.

"I don't think so, Stokes. You're done."

"I wouldn't count on that."

"I would, Stokes."

"A little bitty favor. Or else."

"Or else what?"

"Or else I phone the police."

"And say hi?"

"And tell them who happened to be at Denny Harris's house last night about the time he happened to get murdered."

Ever since talking to his mother and finding out that he'd been late bringing her his treat—a ritual I assumed he treated with utmost respect—I'd wondered where Stokes had been that night.

Maybe I was about to find out.

"Meaning what?" I said lamely.

"Meaning what?" he mocked. "Shit, c'mon, Ketchum, you think I'm some moron?"

"I think you're a lot of things, Stokes, but I guess a moron isn't one of them."

"Hey," he said, "you're really crushing me, you know?" He waved the manila envelope again. "Meaning you were out at Harris's last night, and if I have to, I can prove it."

"Gee, I was always under the impression that when you

71

paid a private detective, he went to work for you. I didn't know that blackmail was a part of the deal."

"Like I said, Ketchum, there's a lot of things you don't know."

What I really wanted to talk about was what Merle Wickes was doing at Stokes's place last night—but I knew better. Despite my naïveté, I was beginning to see that in a sleazy game like this one, the less you said the safer you were. I'd already said and done way too much.

"What's in the envelope?" I asked.

"That isn't important. It's what I want you to do with it that matters."

"Which is?"

"I want you to take this someplace for me."

"Where?"

"You know the duck pond in Bridges Park?"

"Yeah."

"Next to the duck pond there are all these feeders where seed is stored for the birds. The feeders are marked A, B, C, and so forth. I want you to take this envelope and put it in there at a quarter till noon tomorrow."

"What if I look inside?"

"What you see won't make any sense to you."

"I may not be as dumb as you think."

The smirk again. "I'll bet you are, Ketchum, I'll just bet you are."

"Your mommy didn't think so."

Immediately he was tight. "Like I said, leave my mother out of this."

"Nice lady. You must think so, too. Giving up a wife for her."

He flushed. "She was a bitch."

"Mommy knows best."

"I don't really give a damn what you think of me, you

72

know that? All I really give a damn about is you delivering this envelope tomorrow."

"And if I don't?"

"Then I call the police and tell them where you were around the time your partner was murdered."

I put out my hand. He put the envelope in it.

He looked at my face and smiled. "Life's a bitch, ain't it, Ketchum? Right now you look like somebody just injected you with a quart of sour pickle juice."

I tapped the envelope against my fingers. "I assume I'm being used in some kind of blackmail number."

"Mr. Genius."

"I also assume that whoever picks this up is the person who killed Denny."

"You're on a roll. Keep going."

"I also assume that once you get paid off, you'll probably keep right on bleeding them."

"Too bad you didn't kill him, Ketchum. You'd be fun to squeeze." Instead of anger there was now a look of torment in his eyes. For a moment I regretted my ugly crack about his mother.

I nodded to the door. "So long, Stokes," I said. "I'm tired."

"Bridges Park. Quarter to twelve. Feeder A."

He had regained his angry edge. He examined the apartment once more before he left. "Really is kinda nice up here. Maybe someday I'll have a place like it." He smiled. "See you, Ketchum."

TWELVE

When I pulled into my parking space in the morning, Tommy Byrnes swung in a few stalls away.

We met near the exit door leading to our floor.

He smiled. "You in better spirits today?"

I tried hard to smile back. "Sorta, I guess."

"You really had me worried."

The butt-kissing tone was back in his voice. I had probably had Tommy worried about as much as George Bush worries about the derelicts in the Bowery.

I decided to let his bowing and scraping pass.

When you come in from the parking garage, you walk through the art department, which is where in most agencies you find both the highest number of prima donnas and the highest number of everyday, sensible people—the worst and the best.

At 8:23 it was still too early for the prima donnas to be here.

Instead, gathered in the coffee area the artists had made for themselves, stood half a dozen of the people in production, who looked and generally acted more like factory hands than agency types. Which was great as far as I was concerned.

Ab Levin, a sixty-two-year-old World War II veteran who

kept a faded photograph of himself in uniform on his desk and who was probably the best traffic manager in the city, glanced up from his coffee and said, "Talk to you a minute, Michael?"

"Sure," I said.

"Well, see you," Tommy said, walking on.

So much for demonstrations.

"Yeah, Ab," I said, "what can I do for you?"

The other employees looked at Ab, then at me, then back to Ab again. Obviously they'd been talking among themselves.

Ab was a barrel-chested and hairy man whose physical strength belied the extra pounds he'd put on. He always wore clip-on ties. He had shiny black eyes and a voice that sounded sore.

"The people in the back of the shop generally don't hear things right away," he said. "Not usually, anyway. But a couple of us stopped in at The Cove last night and what we heard was . . ." He flushed, seeming embarrassed and ill at ease, as if he were going to tell me he'd betrayed the agency in some way. "Well, we got to drinking, and we got to talking with some people from other agencies and, well, the consensus seemed to be we stood a good chance of losing the Traynor account, now that Denny Harris is dead."

The Cove was a splashy downtown bar where agency people and media types drank. It was the model of the leper colonies I'd mentioned before, the place where both Denny and my ex-wife had spent too many of their hours.

"You really believe everything you hear in the Cove?" I said.

"We're just nervous is all," Ab said. "About our jobs."

Several other people muttered agreement and nodded their heads.

"I mean, to be truthful, Michael," Ab said, "people were wondering if your relationship with Clay Traynor was good

75

enough to keep the account. You know him and Denny catted around a lot—"

My smile must have startled them.

They looked at me with peculiar eyes.

"I wouldn't worry about my relationship with Clay Traynor," I said.

"Yeah, Michael?" Ab said, sounding happily surprised, as if he were about to clap me on the back.

"Yeah," I said. "We had a long talk yesterday and Clay assured me that the account would be staying with us."

The way they looked, I thought they might roll out a pony keg and have a party right on the spot.

I didn't want to spoil their fun by telling them the truth—that the account was staying because of blackmail.

The rest of the morning was much like the scene with Ab Levin. People wanting reassurance that things were going to be all right with the agency—i.e., that we wouldn't lose the Traynor account and fall flat. Advertising is largely a business of rumors, many of which are totally false, but rumors can kill you. Too many of our people spent too many hours in posh dives like The Cove and began to think that the world really was the way it was presented in the dank shadows of the place.

Sarah Anders did something she never had done before—came in late. I wasn't watching the clock because I was angry, rather because I was worried. Having caught Gettig and her on some mysterious mission in Denny's office, and having exposed her affair with Gettig, I was afraid that I'd caused her to do something foolish—like confront her comfortable, suburban husband and tell him that she was in love with somebody else. Even though Sarah was a few years older than I, I felt paternal toward her. People's lives were crazy enough. I didn't want to see hers go the way of all flesh too.

Around ten o'clock she leaned against my doorway and

knocked once. When I looked up, I was staring at a Sarah Anders very different from the one I was used to. My Sarah was always neat, combed, attractive in a matronly way. This Sarah looked as if she'd been up all night drinking beer and watching professional wrestling—her hair was a tumble, her suit unpressed, her makeup blotchy. But that wasn't what I really noticed—that honor went to the blue-gray circle on her right cheekbone, a splotch makeup could not disguise. Either she'd run into something—or somebody had hit her. Given the events of the last few days, the latter seemed more likely.

"Why don't you come in and close the door, Sarah?"

"I should've stayed home today," she said. She sounded as if she were underwater, her voice lost beneath fathoms of fatigue.

"Please," I said, "come in."

I found her a match for her cigarette, a cup of coffee, and my best priestly manner.

When she was all arranged, the first thing she said was, "I wish you'd stop staring at it."

"Sorry," I said.

She sighed. "Here I'm forty-nine years old," she said, "and I'm living out some trashy teenage novel."

I had assumed it was her husband who'd struck her. But something in her tone made me wonder for the first time.

"I just thought I'd like you to know," Sarah said. "I'm quitting. As of right now." Tears silvered her eyes. "Have to, Michael. Have to."

Despite all the puff pieces about the captains of advertising, most agencies worth a damn are run by two or three women who are ostensibly secretaries or executive assistants. The men get the glory, the women do the work. Our agency was no exception. Denny had spent his time keeping Clay Traynor happy, I had spent mine working on the creative product. Neither of us had done what we should. It had been up to Sarah to remind us about appointments, to be sure to keep so-and-so especially happy (usually because she'd learned that another agency was wooing them), and in general see to it that our shoelaces were tied and that we wore clean underwear in case we got hit by a car.

So I had mixed and profound feelings about Sarah's resignation—mixed in that I would miss her personally but even more I would miss her professionally. She ran the damn place, no matter what the names on the door said to the contrary.

"Sarah, why don't you take the next couple of days off?"

She shrugged. "I'll be busy with the funeral, for one thing." She shook her head. She was one of those women who had spent her life being one of the boys—men were comfortable with her in ways they weren't comfortable with other women. She could hear the grossest story, keep the darkest secret, and work the longest hours—without once complaining. The trouble was, this robbed her of a certain humanity. I'd never thought I'd see Sarah sounding or looking like this. I felt pity and a curious kind of disappointment, too, like knowing one of your favorite All-Americans is really a junkie.

"Denny's brother called me last night," Sarah said. "He works for American Express in Europe. He wants me to make all the arrangements and everything."

"Sarah," I said, "why are you quitting?" For now, I didn't want to get sidetracked.

"I couldn't work here anymore with—Ron," she said. The tears started to become sniffles.

"Then Ron won't work here anymore."

"No—" she started to say.

"I've been tired of his whining for years. He isn't half as good as he thinks he is, and his bitching isn't worth the trouble. Whether you stay or not, Gettig's done." I shook my head. "He was one of Denny's drinking cronies anyway. I don't owe him a damn bit of loyalty." I paused. "He's the one who hit you, isn't he?"

She dropped her eyes. Nodded almost imperceptibly.

"What happened?" I said.

She looked up. "You have any whiskey?"

"Sure."

In a minute I handed her a shot of bourbon. Her years as a partner for men had taught her to drink like one—she up-ended the shot glass into her coffee. "Folger's was never this good," she smiled sadly.

The bourbon seemed to help. Something like anger came into her eyes as she started to talk. Much better than the depression and self-contempt that had been there before.

"After you found Ron and me in Denny's office last night," she said, "we went out and had some drinks, deciding what to do next about a lot of things—one of them being us. I was starting to feel terribly, terribly guilty about my husband. Ron's very possessive. The more I talked about my husband, the angrier he got. Finally, I told him that I just wanted it over with."

"That's when he hit you?"

"No, that came a little later, when I said I thought we owed you an explanation about why we were searching Denny's office."

"Why were you?"

"You know, I'm not sure. I'm really not."

For the first time I wondered if I could believe this story. Searching an office without knowing why . . .

"Michael, I'm not lying to you," she said. She had some more coffee, then continued. "Something's been going on the past four months between Denny and Ron and Merle Wickes. Something—I'm not sure what. All I know is that one night the three of them got into a terrible argument and Ron took a swing at Denny. This was in a bar. Things got so

79

bad the bartender threatened to call the police. Nice publicity for the agency, huh?"

"But you don't know what they were arguing about?"

"No. I really don't."

I thought of the photograph Stokes had taken of the person he claimed was the murderer. I wondered if Ron Gettig was going to pick up that photograph this afternoon . . .

"Where does Merle Wickes fit in all this?" I said.

"I'm not sure." She laughed. There was a certain malice in her tone. "Merle Wickes. He's almost pathetic. If he weren't so sad, I mean. He's got such a nice wife and here—" Then she caught herself and laughed again. This time the malice was aimed at herself. "And I've got such a nice husband, right?"

"Yeah, Sarah. He is nice. Damned nice."

She finished her coffee, set it down. "So yesterday, anyway, Ron had me help him look for a box. He said it was about the size of a shoe box. He wouldn't tell me what was in it. At the time I was still wrapped up enough in our sleazy little affair that helping him out sounded like the natural thing to do. Right now, all I want to do is get things back to where they were with my husband."

"Does he know?"

The tears were back. "I think he does, yes. I think he has known the past several months. But whenever he looks at me what I see in his eyes is a kind of pity—not anger or hatred or betrayal. Just pity—as if I don't know what I'm doing and managing to hurt both of us in the process. It's kind of the way he looked at me the night I had our first child—the pity, I mean, the love in that kind of pity. It's understanding, really, not just feeling sorry for somebody. Oh, Christ—" Now she broke down a bit more and gasped a couple times, gasped the dry, clutching reach for tears that won't quite come. There was something ancient in her voice and the way her body bent just now—a middle-aged woman resenting the

80

girl she'd let herself foolishly be. "You got a damn hankie, Michael?" she said when she was finished.

I handed her my handkerchief.

Then I handed her the newspaper clipping.

"What's this?"

"I don't know," I said. "I was hoping maybe you could tell me."

She read it. Shrugged. "I don't have a clue."

"Neither do I." Then I explained how, after she and Gettig had left Denny's office yesterday, I'd found it in a drawer.

"I don't know," she said.

I glanced at my watch. Smiled. "Don't you think it's time you got back to work?"

"But I told you—" she said.

"All you told me is that you're uncomfortable working around Gettig. And I've already told you that problem is about to be taken care of." I pointed to the door. "Now get back out there before I have to start acting like a boss."

Now it was her turn to smile. "I always was a sucker for taking orders." At the door she turned and said, "Thanks, Michael."

THIRTEEN

I spent the next hour feeling a tad of respect for my much-maligned dead partner.

In advertising agencies, it seems, almost nobody gets along. Bosses and supervisors spend nearly as much time refereeing petty squabbles as they do trying to politic their way up the executive ladder. Rivalries are almost as commonplace as adultery. Almost.

For the next sixty minutes, a dozen people, some in couples, some individually, trooped through my office voicing complaints about co-workers. Usually the complaints had to do with turf. One art director didn't like copywriters who went directly to artists without consulting him first. One copywriter wanted to be taken off an account because it wasn't "creative" anymore what with the money-oriented new account exec running it—God forbid we make money. Then there was the paste-up person who wanted to know why he couldn't jog for two hours over his lunch hour—the extra time bound to make him a better worker. Right.

So it went—and that's why I felt some respect for my ex-partner.

Denny Harris had always relieved me of this pain-in-the-executive-butt part of the job. Denny was famous for listen-

82

ing to everybody's complaint, then promptly and forever doing nothing about it. Denny, out of laziness maybe, or maybe even out of real wisdom, believed that if you let things slide along enough they somehow took care of themselves.

I didn't have the stomach for that. My taint was to be combative, as several disappointed-looking people this morning would tell you.

During the last few complaints, my mind started to wander to the manila envelope I had in my car.

I was still in shock that the private detective I'd hired had turned out to be a blackmailer. Stokes made me feel naïve— as if, for all my romantic disillusionment and bitterness, I were some kind of kid. Denny's murder had been shattering enough, but the idea that Stokes was going to feed on Denny vampirelike was even more mind-boggling than the murder.

Which, of course, turned the whole situation right back on me.

Despite the fact that I could tell the police that both the Traynors had been at the murder scene, I did nothing. I was going to save the account—run it up the flagpole and salute my ass off. Which is not the kind of self-image a guy—at least this guy—likes to have of himself. But it was the only way to keep on feeding my family.

The only hope I could see was the newspaper clipping I'd taken from Denny's desk. But I had no idea why he'd kept it—the chances were good that it had absolutely nothing to do with the murder.

This time Sarah Anders didn't scream. All Sarah managed to do, on hearing, was faint.

This time it was one of the women from the copy department who told me. A curt knock on my door moments after my last interviewee of the morning, then: "Mr. Ketchum."

"Yes?"

"You, uh, you better go to the screening room, Mr. Ketchum."

"What's wrong?"

"It's Mr. Gettig."

"What about him?"

"He's dead, Mr. Ketchum. He's dead."

Gettig had been sitting in the darkened screening room looking at outtakes on a videotape machine. Because it was video instead of motion picture, he hadn't needed a projectionist. He'd been alone. Somebody had come in. Down the dark aisle. Apparently very quietly. Put something around his neck and pulled. Very, very hard. In the ugly harsh overhead light, Gettig's neck was a mess, black, blue, yellow, almost amber where blood had bruised along tendons.

He was also a mess in other ways. When you strangle somebody, you not only kill them, you make sure you've humiliated them for whoever has the misfortune to find them. The bowels, you know.

Somebody called the police and somebody else called an ambulance. I wanted to call my travel agent and go someplace. Fast. Far.

Ab Levin put a hand on my shoulder as I turned away from the corpse. He said, "Somebody must hate us, Michael."

At that moment, I didn't understand the significance of what he said. I only nodded dumb agreement. I would have nodded similarly if he'd said that Richard Nixon was a great guy. I'd become a stunned, docile animal.

Around the entrance of the screening room a small crowd had gathered, standing on tippy-toes to peer in, like scared children at a circus tent promising sinister doings inside.

Ab Levin was close on my heels, joining me as I moved down the corridor toward my office.

84

"You got any idea what's going on, Michael?"

"None. Not a goddamned clue."

He put a fatherly hand on my shoulder. "I shouldn't have bothered you earlier this morning."

"Bothered me?" I said, not understanding what he was talking about.

"You know, about the security—our jobs now that Denny is dead."

"Hell," I said, "that's a natural human reaction."

He shrugged, veered off for his own corridor. "Yeah, I suppose. Take care, Michael."

He must have been waiting around the corner for the call, because by the time I crossed my threshold and started for my desk, he was there.

He wore his trench coat again—apparently not bothered by the slight melodramatic flourish it gave to his job as a detective—and exuded the same working-class energy that said he'd probably be happier unloading trucks than all gussied up in a suit and tie. He had his faults, Detective Bonnell did, but there was something straightforward about him that I liked. Or would have liked, if necessity hadn't made me see him as the enemy.

"You're having a bad week, Mr. Ketchum," he said.

"I'm not," I said. "But Denny Harris and Ron Gettig are."

He shook his head. There was something believable about his moment of melancholy. Seeing the kind of human beings he did, and seeing the messes they got themselves in, his melancholy was probably a very civilized reaction.

I went around and sat down and nodded for him to take a chair.

He held up a halting hand. "I've got to join my people in the—screening room is it called?—give them a hand." His gaze held on me a long moment. He was assessing me.

"I've got an alibi for sure this time," I said.

"I know. I've checked. Otherwise things wouldn't look too good for you. From the little checking I've been able to do, I understand you and Gettig almost got into a fist fight the other day."

"Almost is a long way from actually happening."

His gaze hadn't lowered yet. "Sometimes it is, Mr. Ketchum." He waited just the right number of beats—he had good actorly instincts—and then he said, "What's going on up here, Mr. Ketchum?"

"Going on?"

"There's a good probability the murders are related. It would be damned weird if they weren't. So—what's going on?"

"I don't know."

"You're sure of that?"

He almost seemed to be smiling.

"Yeah, I'm sure." I glanced at my wristwatch. Remembered the manila envelope. The delivery. "I have an appointment. Across town. If you don't need me—"

He shrugged. "I'm sure we can handle it, Mr. Ketchum." The pause again. "Do you have any idea who might have killed Gettig?"

"Not really, no." I did, of course. Sarah Anders. Or Sarah's husband—if he'd somehow managed to find out.

He started watching me again. I suppose I don't have the self-confidence needed to take that kind of thing. I could feel tiny beads of sweat start in my armpits.

Then he laid the bomb on me, the one he'd been waiting to deliver, like a terrorist to the heart of an unsuspecting building.

"You know Clay Traynor's wife, Cindy?" he asked.

"A bit. I mean, I see her at agency parties."

"Did she know Denny?"

"Sure."

86

"The same way she knows you? Seeing you at parties?" The mocking edge had returned to his voice.

"Yeah, basically, I guess."

"Then she wouldn't have known him any better than she knows you?"

I sighed. "What is it you're trying to say?"

"Cindy Traynor drives a green Mercedes coupe. I know that because Denny Harris's closest neighbor—maybe half a mile away—remembers seeing a green Mercedes coupe heading for Harris's at dusk. The neighbor was strolling."

"There must be lots of green Mercedes coupes."

"Yeah, but probably not many with the license prefix C-I-N."

This was how it always happens in the movies. Apparently it happens that way in real life, too.

Cindy Traynor was going to get nabbed for the murder of Denny Harris. Clay Traynor was going to find out that his wife had had an affair with Denny.

I was going to lose Clay's account—Cindy might go to prison—and all the while Stokes, the private detective, knew who the real killer was.

"You look nervous, Mr. Ketchum," Bonnell said.

"I'm late," I said, grabbing my briefcase.

And I was—late to do anybody any damned good, including myself.

FOURTEEN

On my way over to the park Ron Gettig's face stayed in my vision. I wasn't much good at this death business. Apparently I wasn't much good at hating, either. Now that Gettig was dead, our dislike of each other seemed petty and silly. For the first time in the five or so years I'd known him, I found myself wondering about his family. All I knew was that he had a wife and daughter downstate someplace. The poor bastard.

I grew up on pop songs about lost summers and early autumns. The city park I looked at now could inspire a whole generation of songwriters—the last red-and-gold leaves tearing away from the otherwise naked trees, the river running through the park peaked with icy-looking waves, the zoo section of the park now just empty cages, the pavilions stacked high with tables and chairs. There was something lonely about all this, you could almost hear the lost laughter of lovers on the bitter wind—but, there, I was writing my own early autumn song.

The duck pond, which I'd expected to be deserted on a snow-promising day like this one, was ringed with maybe half-a-dozen people, all of them looking to be over fifty, tossing bread bits to the ducks that swam by on the other side of the fence. They fed the animals despite a large sign instructing them not to under threat of fine or even imprisonment. The people seemed as imperturbable as the ducks, which, given my mood, buoyed me for a moment. I'm always happy to see people do the right thing despite idiotic laws.

The metal feeder marked A, the one Stokes had instructed me to place the manila envelope in, was wired to the fencing surrounding the pond. It looked like a country mailbox. From inside my overcoat I took the envelope, then placed it inside.

I knew I was being watched.

I glanced around in classic paranoid style but the only people I saw were the well-bundled-up feeders standing around me. A few of them returned my glance, offering smiles and curious looks, but that wasn't what I sensed . . .

I spent the next few minutes looking around. Up the hills that lay westward, the river bank that lay eastward, the forest on the other side of the pond. Somewhere somebody was watching me put the envelope in.

The killer, of course.

I hadn't been able to resist temptation. After Stokes had left last night, I'd carefully opened the envelope and looked inside. All it contained was a photostat of a receipt for a safety-deposit box in the suburb of Millburn. The receipt was signed by a man named Kenneth Martin and had been issued three-and-a-half months earlier.

Stokes had been right. Whatever import the contents held for the person who'd pick them up, I had no idea what they meant or what relationship they had to Denny's murder.

All I knew for sure was that the envelope was going to make Stokes wealthy.

Quarter of a mile away, I found a stand of fir trees and pulled my car over to them. A slope of firs behind it led to the edge of the duck pond. I could stand behind the trees and watch the feeder where I'd put the envelope.

Not an easy jaunt. Several times I slid on the floor of slick fir needles. Another time I caught my overcoat in brambles and had to surgically remove myself from their thorns. But overall there was something thrilling about it, the way I'd felt as a very young boy playing cops and robbers. By now my face was frozen to the point that it was becoming numb—the air was actually starting to become invigorating. If this weren't such a serious business, it would be fun.

I reached the edge of the pond maybe five minutes later, then eased myself out from around the tree to take a look.

I had the terrible feeling that in the seven or eight minutes it had taken me to reach this point, the killer had come and gone.

I decided to wait here as long as I could stand the cold and see what happened.

I didn't have to wait long.

He appeared from behind a copse of trees to the west of the pond. Obviously, he had been watching me.

He went directly to the feeder and took out the envelope.

Then he disappeared.

Quickly.

FIFTEEN

On my desk was a message to call Wilma at a certain number. No last name. Just Wilma. I had my suspicions who it was I would be calling.

An hour after leaving the park, I was still cold. Sarah Anders brought me a large mug of steaming coffee and watched me curiously as I shivered.

"You coming down with a cold?"

"Had a hard time finding a parking place for lunch. I had to walk several blocks."

She smiled. "Must've been very long blocks."

I was staring at her. Obviously. Her lover was less than three hours dead. She seemed to be holding up remarkably well, especially given the fact that her first response on hearing the news had been to faint.

"You're wondering why I'm not hysterical?"

I could feel myself flush. She was a perceptive woman. "I suppose I am."

"Very simple, really. I've decided that I should be more concerned about the living than the dead."

"Meaning?"

"Meaning that I'm going to stay here long enough to make

sure I've collected myself, then I'm going to go home and fix my husband the best meal he's had in years." Tears shone in her eyes. "I've really been a bitch to him."

I decided to help her forget about Gettig by changing the subject. "Did you send everybody home?"

She nodded, pulling herself back from her grief. "Yes. And almost everybody took me up on my offer of the rest of the day off. Only the usual diehards—"

She named several people who were still here.

One of them happened to be the man who'd picked up the envelope at the duck pond.

I could feel my pulse start to pound.

"Why don't you go home now, Sarah?" I said.

"I'm afraid he'll find out someday."

"Even if he did find out," I said, "I'm sure he'd forgive you, if that's what you want."

"Oh yes," she said, tearing up again, "that's what I want, Michael."

I came around the desk and took her in my arms and held her and let her shudder and sob until it passed like a muscle spasm.

"The terrible thing is that I don't feel anything for Ron now," she said. "Nothing at all. I look back on what we did and it just seems—silly. You know?"

These were the words I'd wanted my own wife to speak after she'd told me about her various lovers, including Denny Harris. I'd wanted to patch things up despite my pain and distrust and sorrow, but she hadn't wanted that at all. She'd just wanted out . . .

"Why don't you go home now, Sarah?"

"You really think he'd forgive me if he ever found out?"

I tried to give her an honest answer. I thought of the conversations I'd had with her husband over the years. He was one of those men whose blandness misled people into think-

92

ing he's slow. Actually, he had a quiet, wry sense of humor and what seemed to be a very healthy self-image. He was also obviously ga-ga over his wife of thirty years.

"I think he'd forgive you, Sarah. I honestly do."

This time her tears were punctuated with a kind of laughter. I held her until she pushed gently away and said, "Boy, am I going to fix him a dinner."

The way she said it, I had an image of roast beef and mashed potatoes and peas, my own favorite meal. I half wished she would invite me along.

Twenty minutes later I walked along the corridor leading to the back of the shop.

I still couldn't quite believe that the man I'd seen at the duck pond could actually be the man Stokes planned to blackmail but . . .

On the art department bulletin board I saw a yellowed pencil cartoon of Denny with his leg in a cast being helped into a waiting limousine by Tommy Byrnes. I stopped to examine the cartoon closer. I'd forgotten all about Denny's breaking his leg six months ago playing racquetball, and in fact that Tommy Byrnes had virtually become his valet during that period.

Maybe Denny had said something to Tommy that would shed some light on things. I made a note to contact Tommy later in the afternoon.

A typewriter sounded lonely in the drab afternoon light. As I got closer to the accounting office, the typewriter got louder.

In the reception area, I saw her, sitting alone in an island of empty desks.

Belinda Matson.

She was typing so intensely she didn't notice me until I came up beside her.

Then, startled, she jumped a bit off her seat.

I put what I hoped was a reassuring hand on her shoulder. She wrenched it away as if the hand were poison.

Does nice things for a guy's ego.

"Sorry if I scared you," I said.

Before she spoke, I glanced down at the paper in her type-writer.

The salutation was—"My Dearest Darling Merle—"

It was then that I noticed how tear-stained her eyes looked, and the terrible twitch that traveled through her slight body.

This wasn't a goddamned ad agency, it was a broken-hearts club.

In a gesture similar to shaking off my touch, Belinda put her body across the platen so I couldn't read the paper and said, "I'd appreciate it if you wouldn't pry into my affairs."

Yes, I could certainly read women all right. How had I ever entertained the notion that this woman had any interest in me?

"Sorry," I said. I nodded to the back. "Is Merle in?"

"I'm not sure."

It was so obvious a lie it was almost amusing. She'd said it petulantly, like a displeased little girl. I wondered why she was writing Merle a letter. Maybe she knew something I should.

I just kind of rolled my head in displeasure and walked toward the back, to Merle's office. It was wonderful being boss. You commanded so much respect.

In the gloom I saw a table lamp such as you see in fancy living rooms. Merle's choice in decor was suburban through and through.

I knocked on the curtained glass door. No response. I put my hand on the doorknob. Open. I went in.

In the shadows I saw two things clearly. The body of Merle Wickes seated stiffly in his tall-back executive chair and a glistening .38 sitting in front of him on his desk.

94

I did not need to be a mastermind to know what was happening. Or what was about to happen.

Merle still seemed unaware of my presence. I stood there staring at him, his breathing loud in the gloomy silence, feeling sorry for him, seeing him as a little silly despite the situation and his obvious pain.

It was his hair—that said everything about him. It was silly and I couldn't help it, like taking a Wally Cox type and putting a Wayne Newton hairdo on him and draping him in glitter.

I knew what I had to do. I just wondered if I'd be quick enough to pull it off.

I leaned forward and made a grab for the .38.

Merle surprised me. Completely.

He had the gun in his hand and pointed at me before I had time to lean back.

"Get out of here, Michael," he said. "Or I'll kill you."

"Merle," I said. "It isn't worth it—killing me or killing yourself."

An ugly, self-deprecating laugh came up from him and he shook his head miserably. "You don't know what's going on," he said. "If you did, you'd be scared like I am."

The oddness of his remark almost made me forget that he was holding a gun on me. Here I was assuming that we were talking about his guilt in the two murders, yet he seemed to be saying that he was somehow a victim—

"I'm not following you, Merle."

"Of course you're not. You don't understand a damned thing about what's going on here."

"You mean Denny and Gettig?"

He nodded. "And it isn't going to stop with them." He glanced at the gun. "I'm next. Then probably you."

"Me? What the hell do I have to do with anything?"

He fell back into his miserable silence.

I repeated myself, "What the hell do I have to do with anything?"

"Maybe it's guilt by association." He sounded almost amused.

I wanted to hit him. Hard.

"You went to the duck pond in the city park earlier today," I said. "And the other night I saw you at a private detective's named Stokes."

Instead of shouting out his innocence, or grabbing his gun, Merle Wickes just sat back in his chair and let go with a distinctly asthmatic laugh, a keening little laugh that conveyed a surprising smugness.

"You dumb bastard," he said. "Stokes has got you playing along, I see."

He leaned forward, the laugh still in his voice. "You sure pick good private detectives, Michael. Two days after you hired Stokes, he came to Denny and said that he'd put you on a false trail if Denny paid him enough. To Denny it sounded like a great game. He let Stokes tell you about Cindy Traynor and him just because he knew how much it would scare you—" He laughed again. "You're fun to watch when you get uptight, Michael."

Which was when I grabbed him. Yanked him from behind the desk and hit him so hard across the face that blood spurted from his nose immediately. Then I threw him back in his chair and came around the desk. Any self-confidence his hairdo gave him was gone. He started to whimper and to flutter his hands in front of his face for protection. I couldn't help myself. I grabbed him again and slapped him backhand across the face.

"I want to know what the hell's going on," I said.

"Stokes," he muttered.

"What about Stokes?"

"He's playing us off against each other."

"What the hell does that mean?" I said.

He sat in the chair trying to catch his breath and whimpering and finally he said, "Stokes is bleeding every one of us he can. He found out some things about Denny—and demanded money."

"What things?"

"I—I'm not sure."

"You're a goddamned liar."

"No, really I . . ."

I started toward him again, hating myself for the violence but unable to stop myself, when something hit me on the shoulder.

I groaned, turned to see Belinda Matson standing behind me.

"Leave him alone!" she cried. "He's suffered enough."

I looked at the bronze bookend she'd thrown at me.

The air of violence subsided as we all stood there glaring at each other, not quite knowing what to say.

I was still working on what Merle had said about Stokes, a man I planned to have a talk with as soon as possible.

"Stokes says the photograph you picked up at the duck pond shows that you killed Denny," I said to Merle.

Merle shook his head. "He knows better than that."

"Then you were there that night?"

He shrugged. "Sure I was. I'll even admit we had an argument."

"About what?"

He said nothing.

"About what?"

He sighed. "We had an argument. That's all that matters. But I didn't kill him."

I turned back to Belinda. I wondered if she'd told Merle about Clay Traynor yet and decided she probably hadn't.

And it wasn't my place to inform him that his mistress had a lover.

"Would you mind leaving us alone?" I asked her.

"Yes, I would. I don't want you to hurt him."

"I'm not going to hurt him."

She looked at Merle then at me. "You promise?"

"I promise."

"Is it all right if I leave?" she asked Merle.

He didn't seem to hear her. He was somewhere else.

She stared at him several long moments then left, looking hurt and confused. I wondered what the letter she was writing Merle said. If it admitted to the affair she had had, or was still having, with Clay Traynor, or if it shed any light on the murders. For some reason, I had the feeling that is was a very important letter, and one I needed to lay my hands on.

Merle went back behind his desk and put his hands over his face. Then he took them away. His face looked awful, as if he'd just awakened from the worst hangover of his life.

"There's no way out now," he said.

"From what?" I said, trying to keep my voice friendly.

"You know what I'd really like to do?"

"What?"

"Go back to my wife. Patch things up." He made me think of Sarah Anders—maybe we could have a big group therapy session up here.

"You've got a nice wife."

"Damned nice." He sounded as if he were going to start crying. Then he nodded to the outer office where the sound of a typewriter could be heard. "Clay Traynor strikes again. He and Belinda were seeing each other for a while. Belinda said she just got tired of sitting home alone nights when I had to be with my wife. I guess I can't blame her." But obviously he did.

So he did know. I felt sorry for the poor bastard. Sitting

there, his shoulders slumped, he looked much older than his forty years. In high school, I felt sure, he had been head of the camera club or the science club—the classic nerd as seen by his classmates—and now here he was trying to compensate for all that pain and dislocation by having a hairstyle that looked silly and a mistress who was unfaithful. It wasn't funny. Some of the pity I felt for him crept into my voice. "Why was Denny murdered, Merle?"

He shrugged. "I don't know, Michael, I really don't."

"You didn't do it, then?"

The laugh again. "You really think I could commit murder, Michael?" He was copping to his nerd image—using it to his advantage—but it didn't work. Nerds commit their share of murders, too.

"So why the gun?" I said.

"Because it's all such a goddamn mess, why else?"

"There's something you're not telling me."

He shrugged, sighed again, looked miserable.

I took the newspaper clipping out of my pocket and put it on his desk. Right next to the gun.

He didn't notice it for a while. Then his eyes narrowed and he reached out a delicate finger and picked it up.

The way the blood started filling his cheeky cheeks, it was obvious Merle knew the significance of the clipping.

He surprised me. He decided to lie. He threw it back at me. "Hell, I don't know what this means."

I leaned forward. "Merle, I'm going to hurt you. I really am. Unless you tell me what the hell's going on. What's this clipping got to do with the murders?"

I watched him eye the gun on his desk. Was he thinking of using it on me or himself?

From behind me, a voice said, "You'd better leave now." Belinda Matson.

"I'm not going anywhere."

"Yes, you are," she said, coming into the office. "Because Merle's going to pick up the gun and make you leave." She looked at Merle. "Aren't you, honey?"

Merle flushed again. He didn't want me to see how dependent he was on others for his strength. But that didn't stop him from picking the gun up and pointing it at me. There was oil on the gun and part of the handle was chipped. The flaws made it all the more real.

"You're a stupid bastard, Merle," I said. "There's a good chance you're involved in something that's already taken two lives. But you're not handling it right, believe me. You're going to die, too."

I watched Belinda this time instead of Merle. I could see her pretty, tiny face stretch with anguish as I spoke. Obviously she was worried about the same thing. All these crazy people I was surrounded with—and the secret that tied them all together, the secret I didn't know.

"Merle—" I started to say, feeling sorry for him again.

"All you need to know," Merle said, sounding much more self-confident with the gun in his hand, "is that I didn't kill either Denny or Gettig. Either one of them. Your man Stokes is working a con game—he's got pictures of all of us who were there that night. He was hiding in the house. He decided to fleece me because he wrongly thinks I have access to certain moneys—" He glanced up to little Belinda. She shot him a glance that said he was talking too much. This is how it had been for all of Merle's life. Never quite knowing how to handle a situation, screwing it up more likely than not.

"He'll be clearing out his desk," Belinda said. "He won't be working here anymore. Neither will I."

"That's going to look great to the cops," I said.

She shrugged. Her sense of desperation matched Merle's earlier mood. "They can't prove anything."

100

I stood up. "I wish you two would let me help you."

"You just worry about yourself," Belinda said, now the official spokesperson for both of them. "Whoever's doing this may have you included in the plans, too."

I knew there was no point in asking for that obscure sentence to be cleared up for me.

Merle waved the gun at me again, looking sad and silly.

"I hope you know what you're doing," I said.

"I do," he said. But didn't believe it, either.

SIXTEEN

It took me many long minutes to realize that the hands shaking me were not part of a nightmare but were in fact real.

Ultimately, it was her perfume that convinced me.

She got me up and helped me to the bathroom and held my shoulders as I vomited (and didn't seem at all bothered by the sights or sounds) and then she helped me get into the shower and start the sobering-up process.

According to my watch, it was 8:15 P.M. when I belted my robe, put my feet into slippers, and walked into the living room.

She was curled up at the end of the couch, a diet Coke in one hand, a Ray Bradbury from my bookcase in the other, a jazz interpretation of Kurt Weill's music on the stereo.

"You look a little better than you did an hour ago," she said.

After leaving the office and Merle Wickes, I'd come home and, in a frenzy of self-pity, gotten myself hopelessly drunk.

Her knocking and ringing at the door had awakened me.

I sat down on the couch, rubbing my face. "How are you doing?"

"All right," she said. I just . . ."

When she didn't finish, I looked up. "You just what?"

She smiled. "This afternoon something strange happened to me."

"What?"

"I found myself actually missing somebody. Somebody I really wanted to be around because it would make me feel better than I had in years."

"I hope you're talking about me."

She laughed. "I am."

"I missed you too."

"Why don't I make you some food?"

"I'm not sure what's in the fridge."

"There's bound to be something."

There was. Eggs and bacon and bread for toast. In fifteen minutes I was at the table, eating. She spread jam on toast and ate with me.

"You're watching me," I said after a time.

"Yes."

"I bet I look great. All hungover."

"You look great to me." She flushed. "God, I'm sorry. I mean, I don't want to come on too strong or anything. I mean, I don't know how to do this very well."

With toast in my mouth, I said, "You're doing just fine."

"I really did miss you."

"Me, too."

"I kept thinking, what if it had been you in that library where I'd met Clay all those years ago."

"Would've been nice."

"Do you have anything against Lutherans?"

"Not a single damn thing."

"Do you think we could go to bed?"

"I think that would be swell."

For a while following separation from my wife, I tried the

one-night-stand scene. Not for long. A peculiar loneliness results from sleeping with somebody you scarcely know. At least for me. But then I'm probably doomed to being old-fashioned in many ways. Sex is better for me when I care about someone.

The nice thing with Cindy Traynor was that I cared about her, was starting to fall in love with her.

So I took to bed some long-unsated lust plus a real sense of wanting to know more about the woman, physically as well as psychologically.

Her flesh was silken, the curves of her body tender hollows, the taste of her mouth and the smell of her hair overwhelming there in the darkness. At first there was some awkwardness as I moved down her breasts and stomach but after a few minutes, her breathing sharper, my senses beginning to dizzy, we began making love as if we'd been lovers for years.

She was the right combination for me of sentiment and skill. The things she whispered were as tender as they were sexy, as much about loneliness as need.

There was a lot of thrashing when we both finished within seconds of each other, thrashing and a certain young joy.

Afterward, we lay there listening to each other breathing in the shadows, our hips touching, her cold toes occasionally nuzzling my foot. On the bedroom window I could see snowflakes hit the glass and vanish, big wet flakes making me feel snug inside.

"Do you think you'll get married again?" she said.

"I hope so." I paused. "How about you?"

"I'd really like to be somebody's partner, you know?"

"Yeah. I know. That's what I want, too."

"I really like you, Michael."

"Once all this gets resolved—" I started to say.

She sighed. "I just wish it would get over with. I—asked Clay about it."

104

"You accused him of it?"

"As I said, I think he knew about Denny and me and I think he killed him. I don't flatter myself that Clay has any special feeling for me. It's just his pride." The snowflakes continued to melt and run down the window in rivulets made golden from the parking-lot light below. "Of course," she said, "I'm not positive it was Clay. Actually, it could have been Merle Wickes."

"Merle? Why would he kill Denny? Denny was his idol."

She exhaled smoke. "One night they all came back to our house very late at night. There was Clay and Denny and Ron Gettig and Merle Wickes. They'd all been drinking and there was a lot of noise. They woke me up and kept me up. Finally, I went downstairs to ask them to quiet down. In the den I saw Merle trying to lunge at Denny and take a bag from him. It was a black bag, like a doctor's bag. Denny was drunk and very mean. He kept laughing at Merle, holding the bag out to him, then pulling it back, like a kid's game. Merle kept screaming, 'If I tell what you three have been up to, you're all done.' It should have sounded ominous. The only person who looked upset about Merle was Clay. Clay finally grabbed him and pushed him against the wall and said, 'You're a part of this, Merle, don't forget that. You're a part of this.' Then Clay saw me standing outside the door and really blew up. He told me to get back upstairs."

"But you never found out exactly what was going on?"

"No. Clay closed the downstairs doors. And they kept their voices down. But I wouldn't consider Merle and Denny the best of friends."

"Good. That's what we need."

"What?"

"One more suspect."

She laughed.

"You mind if I turn on the light?" I asked.

"You really want to see me in the nude? I'm not twenty years old, you know."

"Neither am I. If you're self-conscious, cover up."

I turned on the light. She had opted for covering up. I was disappointed.

From my sports jacket draped over a chair I took the newspaper clipping and handed it to her.

It was a brief story:

QUARTER MILLION IN GEMS REPORTED STOLEN

Police report that Mrs. Bradford Amis, wife of financier Bradford Amis, was robbed of more than a quarter million dollars in gems during her recent house party for the March of Dimes.

Police officials were quoted today as saying that Mrs. Amis did not want any publicity on the matter, which is why the three-week-old robbery is only now reaching the press.

Those close to Mrs. Bradford say that the theft occurred even though a private guard had been hired to protect the gems. The guard's name has not been released.

The story went on with more details, none of them seeming to be particularly relevant.

As she read the clipping, Cindy's face looked confused. Then at some point a beautiful clarity came over her face and she smiled. Obviously she had gotten the same idea I had.

"That night downstairs," she said.

"The argument. The doctor's bag," I said.

"But why—?"

"That's the part we don't know exactly—why."

"But we're not even sure they took the gems."

"No, not yet we're not. But I have the feeling if we spend a day or two looking into this thing, we will be."

106

The confusion was back on her face. "But why would they become thieves—Clay and Denny especially? They had very good salaries. I mean, thieves . . ."

I turned out the light.

Any more speculation tonight would be useless.

For now, there were other things to occupy our time.

"I've got to go home in a while," Cindy said, as I leaned toward her in the darkness.

"A while can be a long time," I said.

SEVENTEEN

Even though there was one more funeral to attend—Ron Gettig's—you could tell the shop was getting back to normal by the tone of the arguments I had with several copywriters, art directors, and media directors. Good, hard arguments about the craft of advertising, everything from the tone of copy to the style of illustrations, and whether country-western radio stations were worth the cost-per-thousand they were currently charging. My feeling was, they weren't. There are a lot of guys out there who drive pickup trucks with gun racks in the back, but how many of them do you really want to talk to unless you're selling chewing tobacco or beer?

I even managed to get some writing done on the Traynor account, which, despite everything that had happened, still paid the majority of salaries and bills around here.

Each time I typed the name Traynor I thought not of chain saws but of Cindy. I felt giddy in a way I hadn't in a long time. I'd picked a damned strange time to fall in love—but so be it. The taste of Cindy remained in my pores. It tasted great.

I didn't even think any more about checking out the newspaper clipping with Mrs. Bradford, the one who'd been robbed. All I could think of was Cindy . . .

That changed when Sarah Anders knocked on my door to tell me Detective Bonnell was in the reception area. Sarah saw the expression on my face and frowned. "It isn't over yet, is it?"

"No," I said, not sure what she meant.

She closed the door by leaning against it. This morning she looked the suburban matron. There was a mellowness in her mood I hadn't seen for a long time. "I had a long talk with my husband last night."

"You told him about Ron?"

"No. Not exactly. What I did tell him was how much I loved him, and how sorry I was that sometimes I acted so distant. I'm not sure he knew exactly what I was talking about but by the time we finished talking both of us felt better—I could tell."

A measure of how paranoid the murders had made me was that I began picturing Sarah's husband as a suspect. It is not a good way to live . . .

"I'm happy for you," I said.

"I just wish you looked better."

"Tired?"

"More than tired, Michael. The strain . . ." Apparently my air of puppy love wasn't reflected on a face with dark rings under the eyes and the paleness that comes from too much alcohol and too little sleep.

"I'll be all right," I said.

The way she looked at me, I thought maybe she knew something terrible about my health that I didn't.

"I hope so," she said.

When she opened the door, Bonnell was standing there, still looking uncomfortable in a suit and tie. He came in with an earnest but enigmatic expression on his hard face. He put out his hand and I shook it. He sat down. Before my bottom reached my own chair, he said, "I wanted to tell you that I'm about to make an arrest in both murder cases."

"What?" My surprise was genuine.

He smiled. "Most murder cases aren't nearly as complicated as the press makes them out to be. Especially once you've established a motive."

I asked him if he wanted any coffee. He said sure enthusiastically. I got up and got him some. I wished for a bourbon and water but knew better.

I sat back down again.

He thanked me for the coffee and went on. "You ever hear of a Mrs. Bradford Amis?" he said.

"No," I lied. I was afraid my face was saying otherwise.

"Five months ago, she had nearly a quarter of a million dollars in gems taken from a wall safe in her home. She was having a party for charity. A lot of fancy society types were there, including your good friend Clay Traynor." He said "good friend" with his usual irony. "Guess who was also with him? Denny Harris and Ron Gettig."

"I'm not following you," I said. But my attempt at sounding stupid wasn't convincing to either of us.

"What if Traynor and Harris and Gettig got themselves invited to that party so they could take the gems?" he asked.

"Do you know who you're talking about? I mean, they're hardly the thief type."

"What's the 'thief type,' Mr. Ketchum? I don't think there is such a thing—especially when somebody is desperate."

"What did they have to be desperate about?" I was thinking of my conversation with Cindy. "Clay Traynor has a very good income—so did Denny and Gettig."

"You think so, huh?"

From his pocket he took a thick fold of papers. When he spread them out on the desk before me, I saw that they were bank and financial statements from a variety of sources.

"Here we have the financial status of the three men we're talking about," Bonnell went on. "When you give these reports a superficial look, everything seems all right. But when you look closely, you see that all three of them were deeply in debt."

He pushed the papers over to me.

Five minutes later, after having looked through everything, I saw that what he said was true. Everything from failed business ventures to expensive cars had put each man deeply, and perhaps irrevocably, in debt. What was most interesting was that two or three of the business ventures—a marina and a parts-supply house for foreign cars—they'd been in together, Clay, Denny, Ron Gettig. I realized it was time I contacted my personal accountant again—he was going through the agency books at night.

"Still think they didn't have motive enough to commit a robbery?"

"All right," I said, "I'll grant you motive, but how about actually doing it. They liked to play hard, but I still say they weren't criminal types. Anyway, how would they know how to break open a safe?"

He smiled. "I've been a busy man, Mr. Ketchum. I've got answers for every question."

I found myself smiling with him. He seemed to take a real delight in his work. But I didn't know what I was smiling about. If he booked Clay Traynor, events would set in motion the eventual—and probably sooner than later—transfer of power from Clay to his cousin, and the transfer of the account from Harris-Ketchum to some other agency.

No, I didn't have anything to smile about. My early morning mood of puppy love was fading fast.

"They didn't know how to break open a safe," Bonnell said, "but a security guard named Kenneth Martin did."

This time, I felt myself literally rise up from the chair. I was aware of Bonnell watching me closely. Instant sweat pasted my face and armpits.

Bonnell had indeed been busy.

"You all right?" he said.

111

I shrugged. "Didn't sleep very well last night. Upset stomach."

He held my eyes momentarily, enigmatically, then went on.

"I have warrants out for the arrest of both Clay Traynor and this man Kenneth Martin. I think I can prove that Harris and Traynor met Martin a few months before the party, got him planted in the security job, and had him help them steal her gems. Kenneth Martin has been around—never quite in prison but busted enough times for minor things that he might very well be able to pick a safe if he was offered enough money."

"Sounds like a bad movie."

"You've never heard of Kenneth Martin?"

I thought of the receipt in Stokes's blackmail envelope. I thought of Merle Wickes claiming the envelope. The receipt had been signed by one Kenneth Martin.

"You say you can prove all this?"

"I'm a careful man, Mr. Ketchum. I said I *think* I can prove all this. At the very least, I have enough circumstantial evidence to make an arrest of both Clay and Martin." He shook his head.

"I wanted to warn you about the arrest," Bonnell was saying. "Give you a little time to prepare yourself for the publicity about a client of yours killing your partner and one of your producers." He smiled. This time it wasn't a pleasant smile. "I also wanted to give you a chance to do a little rewriting."

"Rewriting?"

He sipped his coffee, trying to be as casual as possible. "Yeah. A few days ago you gave me a story about being with Clay Traynor the night Denny Harris was murdered. I thought in light of everything that's happened, you might want to do a little revision on that story of yours."

112

So there we were.

This wasn't the courtesy call I'd almost believed it to be. On the contrary, Bonnell was going to recruit me to do the one thing absolutely necessary to hanging Clay Traynor and losing the Traynor account in the process—break Clay's alibi.

"Well," he said, after a minute or two of my silence, "how about it, Mr. Ketchum? Was Clay with you the night of Denny Harris's murder?"

Just then—proving incontrovertibly that God is in fact up there watching over me—the intercom buzzed.

Sarah said, "Sorry to interrupt but there's a problem in production, Michael. Ab Levin just hit Tommy Byrnes and hit him pretty hard."

I swore, wondering what the hell was going on back there. My world had become one of the insane terrains you walk across with a rifle slung across your back and your hands filled with grenades.

"I'm sorry," I said to Bonnell, "would you mind if I find out what's happening back there? My agency seems to be disintegrating right before my eyes."

He stood up, looking very understanding. "Sure, it's all right, Mr. Ketchum."

I interrupted him before he could say anything else. "If you could just wait here—"

"That isn't necessary," he said.

I started around my desk.

He grabbed my arm.

"All I need is a simple yes or no answer," he said.

I looked longingly at the door. I would be happy to go in the back and referee a match between Ab Levin and Tommy Byrnes. I would be happy to spend a month or two in a leper colony. Anything—but answer Bonnell's question.

"How about it," he said, as if I had managed to forget what

113

he'd asked me. "Was Clay Traynor with you the night that Denny Harris was murdered?"

I stared at him. He stared at me.

"They really need me in the back—" I said.

He smiled. "Yes or no, Mr. Ketchum. Then you can go." He paused. "Yes or no. Mindful of perjury laws. Perjury can be a very nasty business."

I knew what I had to say, knew that despite the evidence Bonnell seemed to have, I had to continue my risky poker hand.

"He was with me right up until midnight," I said. "Right up until midnight."

What surprised me was the look of disappointment on his face. He seemed to take my moral failings personally—as if I'd betrayed a real friendship we'd had.

"Yeah," he said sadly. "Sure he was."

He didn't wait for me to say goodbye.

EIGHTEEN

By the time I reached the production area, a small group of people stood between Ab and Tommy. The glares the two exchanged, however, spoke of an argument still smoldering.

The general air was of melancholy. In the moments following a blowup, most men I know tend to fall into a kind of remorse. Maybe they're thinking of just how bad things could have gotten—that instead of some harsh words being exchanged, or even a few stray punches, there could have been real bloodshed.

Given two murders in the past few days, I'm sure that thought was not uncommon.

At Tommy's feet lay a piece of rope curled around like a snake in waiting. Everybody was careful not to get too close—as if it were radioactive.

"You think we could break it up?" I said. I looked at the half-dozen production people standing around—dressed more like warehouse workers in jeans and work shirts and flannel shirts—and shook my head. "I know the past few days have been tough for all of us, but we've got to get the work out no matter what."

There was no resentment on their faces as they started to

disperse—only a kind of curiosity directed at Ab and Tommy.

Bill Malley, one of Ab's assistants said, "What Ab says is true, Mr. Ketchum. Honest."

Then Malley, with the rest of the men, went back to their area.

"What's true?" I asked Ab.

The man looked miserable, as if he were carrying around a secret so terrible it was literally destroying him. He said nothing, only stared at the rope, then glared up at Tommy. But there was more than anger in Ab's gaze—I saw the same expression that had been in Detective Bonnell's a few minutes earlier. There was disappointment in Ab's eyes.

"What's true, Ab?" I repeated.

"Aw, nothin'," Ab said. "I must've made a mistake is all." He turned and started away but I put out a hand and stopped him.

"Ab, I want to know what's going on here. You and Tommy disrupted the whole department. I think I've got an explanation coming."

Tommy, his Norman Rockwell face flushed, said, "I'll tell you what's going on."

He motioned to the rope on the floor.

"Ab decided to sneak some candy," Tommy said, "the way he usually does." A kind of fondness softened Tommy's voice momentarily—Ab and Tommy were father-son, Ab always sampling the candy Tommy kept in his desk. "Anyway, when he dug in my desk drawer he found the rope. I guess he thought . . ." The flush on Tommy's face grew deeper. Tormented. "He thought he'd found the rope that had been used to strangle Ron Gettig."

I glanced at Ab. His eyes were still downcast.

Tommy went on. "So he asked me about it—about the rope and everything, and when I told him I hadn't ever seen it before, he got mad and said I would only make things worse by lying." Tommy's voice gained an octave. "Honest, Michael, I've never seen this rope before. Somebody put it there!"

"Bill Malley," Ab said, speaking at last. "He saw me pull the rope out of Tommy's desk. He knows it was in there."

"Sure it was in there, Ab," Tommy said. "But somebody put it there—planted it there, can't you see that?"

Ab shook his head. "Aw, that's just in movies, Tommy. I saw you and Gettig arguing that day! Just tell the damn truth, that's all."

I glanced at Tommy. "What were you and Gettig arguing about?"

"Just because we were arguing doesn't mean I'd kill him," Tommy said, sounding very young, almost hysterical. "God, I . . . I couldn't kill anybody."

The whole idea of murdering somebody sounded preposterous to Tommy—as it seemed to at that instant to Ab Levin.

He smiled at Tommy. Suddenly. Surprisingly. "You're right."

Tommy smiled nervously in return. "Last time I killed anybody, Ab, was in a fantasy I had a year ago when another guy took my girlfriend."

I was glad they were getting along again, but Tommy still hadn't answered my question about Gettig and why they were arguing.

"Ab, you mind if Tommy and I speak alone?" I asked.

Ab's first response was suspicion. "Hey, the thing about the rope, that's all cleared up, right?"

"Right," I said. Then I saw that he wanted me to explain why I wanted to talk to Tommy. You pay a price for having a democratic managerial style. "I want to find out why he and Ron Gettig had an argument."

Ab said, "I'm curious myself."

Looks like I had company.

Tommy said, "About a week ago some videotapes Ron had wanted arrived—sample reels from various production companies. The package came and I took it in and put it on his desk. He came in and got all bent out of shape, like he was hiding something and I'd discovered it."

"That must've been when I came in," Ab said.

"Yeah, it was," Tommy said.

"I thought he was going to hit you."

"Yeah, so did I."

"*Did* you happen to find anything in his desk?" I asked.

"God," Tommy said, "what a day. First Ab accuses me of being a killer, and now you're calling me a thief."

"Tommy," I said, "all I meant was did you find anything that looked suspicious lying around on his desk. He's been murdered. We're trying to find out who did it and why. I thought maybe you'd seen something that could help the police."

Ab clapped a hand on his shoulder. "It's all right, kid. We're all just a little jumpy."

"Yeah," Tommy said, "I guess so." He shrugged. "Nah, I didn't see anything suspicious, Michael."

"And Gettig didn't give you any hint of what he might be trying to conceal."

"Uh-uh."

I sighed.

Ab and Tommy caught the significance of the noise I made.

"No offense," Ab said, "but you look like heck, Michael. I mean you got bags under your eyes that could hold three days' worth of laundry."

"Thanks," I said, trying to laugh.

The wide fatherly hand left Tommy's shoulder and came down on mine.

"You get some rest," he said. "Otherwise you ain't going to be worth a damn to anybody."

But I was no longer paying attention to Ab. Instead I was looking at the man in the dark raincoat and the dark fedora who stood in the doorway. The big man with the air of comic menace. My favorite private eye, Stokes.

Ab caught the line of my gaze and quit talking. His eyes followed mine over to Stokes. He had the same reaction I had on first seeing Stokes—his eyes narrowed, trying to pinpoint the elusive reason that Stokes should exude such an air of evil.

Maybe I was imagining things, but I thought I saw Ab shudder.

That was when I noticed how pale Tommy had gotten.

Stokes had fixed the kid in his gaze. Tommy danced nervously, as if on the point of a knife.

A yellow grin twisted Stokes's mouth. If the agency was ever called on to do a poster against child molesting, I knew who we could cast in the role of the villain.

Tommy, clammy now, said, "Maybe I'd better be getting back to work, Michael."

"Interrupting something, am I?" Stokes said, strolling in the room.

Ab said, "Yeah, I better get back to it, too, Michael." He reached over, clapped Tommy on the back, and the two started away.

So it wasn't just me. A lot of people had the same repelled response to Stokes.

"You make friends everywhere you go," I said.

Stokes laughed. "I quit worrying about friends when I was in second grade."

Stokes bent down and picked up the rope. "I read in the paper where your man Gettig was strangled."

In his black-gloved fingers, the ordinary piece of clothesline rope assumed a violent significance. "Interesting," he said.

"What do you want, Stokes?"

119

He looked at the rope then let it drop back to the floor.

From inside his black coat he took a piece of paper. A newspaper clipping, much like the one I'd been carrying around myself these past few days, flared from his fingers.

"I want you to come by my office tonight at ten o'clock," he said. "I think I've figured this thing out for you. I can save you some headaches—and maybe your life."

He smiled yellowly again.

"The way you tried to save Merle Wickes's life," I snapped. "By blackmailing him?"

"So you peeked, huh?" he said, greatly amused that I'd looked inside the manila envelope he'd had me drop off at the duck pond the other day.

"I had a right to see what was going on."

"Don't get pious," he said. "You peeked just like everybody else would—just like I would." He chuckled. I had confirmed his suspicions that human beings were a sorry lot.

"Merle didn't do it."

"No, he didn't. But he's involved and he's got access to money—money I could use."

"Merle?" I said. "Money? You're crazy."

Stokes's eyes swam angrily behind his thick glasses. "I didn't say his money. I said access to money. I don't care whose money I get, I just need some."

For the first time—a curious tone of pleading, of desperation, in his voice—Stokes sounded human. It didn't make him any more pleasant, it just took the spooky edge off him.

"I want you at my office tonight at ten o'clock," he said. The threat had come back in his voice.

He handed me the newspaper clipping he'd been holding.

"See you," he said.

NINETEEN

She called around lunchtime. When I heard her voice, the receiver seemed to glow. All kinds of sappy lines came to mind when I started to talk, but I was afraid to say them, afraid to make myself vulnerable in case she'd been using me the way she'd been using Denny and decided to drop me.

"I'm still thinking about last night," Cindy Traynor told me. "You're really sweet."

"Gee," I said, "a guy likes to be told he's handsome or strong or bright, but I'm not sure he likes to be told he's sweet."

She laughed. "If he really understands women, then he knows how much of a compliment that is."

Now I laughed. "OK, I'll take your word for it."

"Detective Bonnell, the one you told me about, he was here this morning."

"Here?"

"My home. Questioning Clay. From the little I could hear, I think he thinks Clay did it."

"He didn't arrest Clay, did he?"

"No, but from what Clay said, he came pretty close." She paused. "Clay's not holding up very well. He started drinking bourbon straight after Bonnell left, then he went out. I'm not sure where. I'm worried about him and—and I think he may actually have done it."

"What makes you think so?"

"Remember I told you about the night Gettig and Merle Wickes and Clay were here and Denny was trying to get the bag from Merle?"

"Yes?"

"Guess what I found?"

"What?"

"The bag."

"Yeah?"

"Yes, tossed in among some stuff to be carried out that for some reason never got carried out."

"Anything special about the bag?"

"Yes. There's only half of an identification tag on the handle—as if it got torn off."

"Maybe I'd better take a look at the bag."

She laughed.

"What's so funny?"

"You," she said. "Sometimes you sound so earnest. 'Maybe I'd better take a look at the bag.' Sherlock Holmes."

"This is my day to sound earnest and pious," I said, thinking of Stokes's crack. "Can you get away for a drink around five or so?"

"Sure," she said. "I don't expect Clay back. When he starts drinking like this, he usually winds up at his honey's. Whoever she happens to be at the moment."

There was faded anger and regret in her voice. For a second I was jealous. I didn't want her to feel anything for Clay, even if the emotion was faded.

"Around five, then?" she said.

I named a place.

Three hours later I was sitting in my office going through storyboards when the phone buzzed.

Sarah said, "Mr. Hauser from Hauser Accountants is on the line."

"Fine," I said. I punched him in immediately. "Hello," I said.

"How about this weather?" he said. "I think I'm heading for Florida."

Great, just what I wanted. He was charging me two hundred dollars an hour to audit my profit-and-loss sheets and he was spending his time on the most banal of amenities.

I realized, of course, that I was overreacting—I was too eager to find out what was going on.

"Well," I said, "did you find out anything?"

"Maybe I have," he said.

Then again, I thought, maybe you haven't.

I said, after he said nothing, "Care to tell me about it?"

"Are you familiar with Eagle Productions?"

"Eagle? No, I don't think so."

"Apparently they produce TV commercials. They're located in Kansas City."

I thought hard. We used a variety of production houses for our commercials and product songs, including production houses in Kansas City. But I'd never heard of Eagle Productions and, as creative director, I was the logical one to know the name.

"Why are you asking me about them?" I said.

"Well," he said, "I'd rather finish running some things down before I say."

"Wonderful," I said, "just what I need. A cliffhanger."

"Beg pardon?" he said.

"Nothing. Call me back when you're ready to talk."

"You bet I will," he said, all enthusiasm. "Thanks for your time."

As I hung up, there was a timid knock on my door. I called out for whoever to come in.

Tommy Byrnes entered.

123

"I talk to you a minute?" he said.

"Sure," I said.

He nodded to the door behind him. "All right if I close the door?"

"Sure."

He came over to a chair and set himself down. In the fading light of the gray day he did not look so young, and certainly not so happy.

For the first time since I'd known him, I saw him fidget with his long, slender fingers.

"That guy in the black overcoat who came in," he began.

"Yes?" I said. Then I remembered his particularly violent reaction to Stokes—the way he'd gone pale and seemed to lose his composure.

"I saw him one night with Ron Gettig—one night in the Cove. There was something about him . . ." Tommy shook his head. "I mean, I'm not saying he had something to do with all this but—"

"Kind of a creep, isn't he?" I said.

"Yeah. He scares me. He—I wouldn't put nothin' past him. Nothin'."

I leaned forward on my desk. "Is there something you want to tell me, Tommy?"

"Yeah. Kinda. You remember when Denny broke his leg and I kinda had to chauffeur him around?"

I nodded.

"Well, one day he asked me to drive him out to this place—this mansion, actually—and I saw the guy in the black overcoat there, too."

The word mansion reminded me of the clipping Stokes had handed me. Though it was from a different newspaper than the clipping I had, it detailed the same robbery at Mrs. Bradford Amis's.

He stood up. "I was kind of scared to tell you. The way that guy looked at me this afternoon—"

124

"You should have told me before, Tommy."

"I didn't think it was important, I guess." He nodded to the door. "Well, I've got a class in a couple hours. Copywriting. I've gotta get ready for it." He stared at me. "You, uh, you aren't mad, are you?"

"No," I said. "No, I'm not, Tommy."

He smiled. Up in heaven, Norman Rockwell would be very pleased. "Good," he said, and pulled his stocking cap on his head.

"Well," he said, "guess I'll take off, then."

"Fine," I said, scarcely aware of him.

He went out.

TWENTY

The Devon was a bar in the downstairs of a hotel that had been fashionable thirty years ago. Somehow management had kept the bar in good shape while letting rats and winos roam the upper floors. It was possible, in the dim glow showing racks of liquor bottles, in the brocaded wallpaper that gave the bar a British feel, to hear the echoes of big-band music, and to hear excited men talk about Musial's latest home run while they puffed on Chesterfields.

Cindy waited for me in the shadows near the rear. Tonight she wore a gray tailored suit, with her shining blond hair swept up on the right side. With her glossy lipstick, and the cigarette burning in the ashtray, she seemed to belong in this bar haunted by the forties.

After I'd sat down and ordered a martini, Cindy reached down and picked up the bag next to her. She was right—it did look like a doctor's bag.

"So this is the famous bag," I said.

She shrugged. "Disappointed?"

I smiled. "Sort of. I guess I hoped to find a note inside."

"A note?"

"Yeah. One explaining who killed Denny Harris and Ron

126

Gettig, and what Merle Wickes knows that he isn't telling me about this black bag."

She laughed. "Gee, that would be a long note."

"It could be much longer. It could go on to tell me what a private eye named Stokes knows about your husband, and why somebody planted a piece of rope in Tommy Byrnes's desk this afternoon, trying to make it look like Tommy had strangled Gettig."

She glanced up as the waiter set our drinks down.

When I looked back at her she was staring at her drink as if it were a crystal ball. I didn't need to ask whom she was thinking about.

"They're going to arrest him," she said, obviously referring to her husband. Her voice had gotten raw suddenly, as if she'd just developed a sore throat.

"Maybe they won't," I said.

She stared glumly into her drink. "I feel guilty."

"Why?"

"Because the police seem to be focusing on him. And here I am enjoying myself with a man whom I like a great deal."

I touched her hand. "We don't know for sure that he's the killer."

"Maybe the real killer won't ever be found but the police will blame him anyway." She frowned. "Poor Clay." I leaned over and kissed her cheek.

She turned and our lips touched.

After we went back to our drinks, she said, "What kind of sweaters do you like?"

"Crew necks, I guess, why?"

"Would you mind if I knitted you one?"

"That'd be great."

"I'll start tomorrow."

"Thank you."

"No, thank you, Michael. I enjoy a sense of being needed."

I stared at the bag sitting on the edge of the table. "Speaking of needed, I need to know how this bag fits into everything."

I pulled it over, started inspecting it.

Up close, the bag looked cheap, leatherette instead of leather. The name tag was one of those clear plastic window jobs encased in a leatherette oblong. Except the oblong had been torn in half. What remained of the tag were two lines of writing—or rather two half lines of writing.

07 107th St.
0307

There is a 107th Street in the city, but there are 107th Streets in lots of cities. The big problem is the 0307—the tag was smudged enough that I couldn't tell if those were the last digits of a zip code or a phone number. If it was a phone number, it would take a long time to run down.

"Any brainstorms?" she said.

"This tag looks like a phone number."

"How could we ever find out the first digits?"

"There are four prefixes in the city's phone system."

"Right."

"What if I put them in front of the numbers we have and start dialing. Maybe we'll get lucky."

"That sounds as if it will take a long time."

"They've got two phones in the back. If you take one and I take one, we can cut the time in half."

"When do we start?"

"How about now?"

By six o'clock the snow and the cold had filled the bar with people wanting to get warm and have some laughs and discover the secret of immortality.

128

We were in our respective phone booths, the ten dollars in dimes we'd bought laid out before us. Thus far I'd had no luck. The formula had gotten me nothing but polite sorrys, impolite and irritated (lots of people seem to be either sleeping or having sex at this time of evening) NOs, or courteous old people who want to help me find whoever it is I'm looking for but don't have a clue as to how I should go about it.

I checked with Cindy. She was having no more luck.

About the time a big guy who looked as if he'd recently forsaken his job as a lineman for the Packers and had taken up selling insurance started hovering around the phone booth—about that time something unexpected and wonderful happened.

I added an eight to the formula, heard the female voice say "Beloit Motel." I described the bag. Tensely, the woman on the other end of the phone said, "Mister, maybe you'd better come right out here."

TWENTY-ONE

The Beloit was the kind of motel you expected to find on the edges of an industrial park, a large plastic box that had once been white but that was now, and irrevocably, stained by the elements and the pollution that hung on the air like gauze.

The snow made the place look better than it should have, the cracked windows warmer with light, the filthy sidewalk white.

The office was located on the ground floor right of the building.

As I opened the door, the acrid smell of a greasy, burning dinner lunged at us like a rabid dog. I could see Cindy's features crumble in displeasure. My stomach turned once.

The cooking was being done on a tiny gas stove. I didn't want to know what she was actually cooking—the contrast between the relatively fresh cold air outside and the cloying smell in here was enough.

She turned to us without smile or frown on her face, just a kind of idle stare, as if she were a robot that was voice-activated.

"Are you Mrs. Kubek?" I asked, knowing she was.

She wiped strong hands against her faded housedress.

Nodded. "Yes," she said. "If you want to call me that. Husband's been dead now twenty years." She had a face and body and manner that hard work had beaten into weary submission years ago. Probably she was in her mid-forties. She could have passed for sixty, an unhealthy sixty.

"I wonder if you'd show me Kenneth Martin's room."

At the mention of the man's name something small but wonderful happened to Mrs. Kubek's face. A suggestion of happiness lit the eyes and turned the corners of the mouth into a smile. Momentarily, at any rate. Then the weariness came back, coupled now with a strong sense of disappointment, and she nodded her graying head toward the outdoors.

"Police came three months ago," she said. "I called 'em after he didn't show up for a week. That wasn't like him at all. He's a man who likes three meals a day and a quart of beer in the evening and an hour or two of television before he goes to bed. He's not a drifter." She used the word as if it described the worst kind of degenerate imaginable. In her business, it probably did.

While she spoke, more to herself, really, than to us, I glanced at Cindy.

She looked alternately moved and put off by this woman. When I nudged her, and she angled her head toward me, I saw that there were the beginnings of tears in her eyes.

Suddenly the cubicle-office got oppressive to me. I wanted to be outdoors again in the relatively fresh, cold air—away from the numbing sense of loss in the room and the stench of greasy food.

"Could I see his room?" I asked.

For the first time Mrs. Kubek seemed suspicious. "I still don't understand why you called. You're not with the police?"

I shook my head.

"And you ain't with that other fellow?"

"What other fellow?"

131

She made a face. "Guy with real thick glasses. Always wears a black topcoat."

My good friend Stokes-the-creep.

"When was he out here?" I asked.

She smiled. "Oh, several times."

The smile was odd, made me curious. I had to wait for her to explain.

"First time he was out here," she said, "I kinda surprised him." Dramatically, she leaned behind the registration counter. In moments she produced an impressive-looking revolver. "With this."

"He was breaking in?"

She nodded. "Yeah. He'd helped himself to Kenneth's room. Let himself in. I happened to be taking something down the hall to one of the other rooms. I went back and got my gun here and surprised him. He was scared, let me tell you." The smile was back on her face. I realized then that there was at least the possibility that Mrs. Kubek was not quite right. What I'd put down to grief might well be insanity of some kind.

"Could I see the room?" I said.

"You never answered my question, mister."

I shrugged. "Some terrible things have been happening to people I know lately."

"Like what?"

"Two of them have been murdered."

If the subject of murder made much impression on Mrs. Kubek, she didn't show it.

"So why do you want to see Kenneth's room?"

"Because he might have known something about the killer."

"Why would you think that?"

I stared at her. "Believe it or not, we're trying to help you."

She seemed to think this over, that we could be friends. "Wait outside."

132

"What?"

"Wait outside."

I shrugged.

When the door swung shut behind us, the hard cold night air began seeping into my bones. It felt great. I watched my breath plume against the night sky and listened to the rumble of semis in the distance and stared briefly at the brilliant stars.

"Thinking about anything special?" Cindy asked, leaning into me, smelling wonderfully of perfume, liquor, and her own body warmth.

I hugged her to me.

"Just sometimes, looking up at the stars . . ." I didn't want to finish it.

She snuggled up to me. "I know. It makes you think about God, doesn't it?"

"That's the weird thing. I'm not religious in the formal church way. All the man-made wrangling gets me down." I stared up at the stars, recalling from my boyhood Edgar Rice Burroughs's John Carter novels and the fateful sense Burroughs gave the winking stars. In his way, Burroughs had been a very religious writer, and in a far more persuasive way than many church-approved ones. "But sometimes . . ." I laughed. "Maybe hanging around Lutherans is good for me."

Cindy hugged me again. Invitingly. I wanted to be in bed with her, warm and floating on the cadences of her soft voice.

Behind us, the door opened.

Mrs. Kubek shuffled into the night beneath a worn gray topcoat. Men's buckle boots covered her legs halfway up to her knees. A faded scarf covered her head. A fistful of keys dangled from her fingers. She didn't say anything, she didn't even nod any acknowledgment. We followed her.

Half an hour later I sank down on a mattress that was not much thicker than a slice of bread.

Kenneth Martin's room had the feel of a man who spends his time existing rather than living. From the pinup-style calendar (the girls busty but clothed) to the plastic statue of Jesus on the dresser to the neat stack of *Reader's Digests* next to the frayed armchair, here were the remnants of a man who had imposed a kind of civilization on an otherwise dreary life. His pride would be that he was clean, punctual, dependable. He would not worry about other people's opinions of him but rather his own opinion of himself. When I looked around the room, I saw what had probably attracted Mrs. Kubek to him. In her world of drifters, winos, and grinning traveling salesmen, there was a real working-class dignity to Martin.

The trouble was, while his room suggested many things about his personality, it told me nothing about his possible involvement in the robbery of Mrs. Bradford Amis, and what he might know about the murders that followed.

I opened the drawer in the nightstand next to the bed. Inside was a prayerbook, a pack of stale gum, and a western paperback. I thumbed through the book. A black-and-white photograph fell out. I judged the picture to be maybe fifteen years old. The two men in the photo wore the flowered shirts of the mid-sixties and their sideburns were long and wide. They stood in front of a tiny frame house on the side of which sat two rusting-out cars. There might have been a white-trash sense of the men and the place except for the scrupulous order and cleanliness of them, the house, and even the rusted cars. On the steps of the house, almost out of focus, sat a small boy and a woman.

I held the photo up to Mrs. Kubek. "Are either of these men Kenneth Martin?"

She took the photo. Examined it. "The one on the right. That's Kenneth."

Tears were in her eyes.

"You know who the other man is?"

134

"His brother, Don."

"You know how I could contact him?"

She shook her head. "Can't."

"Why not?"

"Dead. Him and his wife. That's her in the back, the wife. Traffic accident. Sometimes when Kenneth drank . . ." She shook her head. "Well, sometimes he'd talk about the accident and he'd get real depressed. Then he wouldn't talk at all. A family like that—wiped out. It don't make no sense, does it?"

I put the photo back into the book and the book back into the drawer. I was beginning to feel that I was violating a living, breathing entity by being here.

I glanced over at Cindy. She was fingering a doily on the bureau, looking as blue as I was starting to feel.

"What about Stokes, Mrs. Kubek?" I asked. "Did he say why he was here?"

"Not really. Just said he was working on a case and he thought maybe Kenneth could help him clear it up."

"He didn't have any idea where Kenneth was?"

She shrugged. "He said he'd never even met Kenneth. Just working on a case."

"He didn't say what case?"

"Uh-uh."

Stokes. The bastard was everywhere, seemed to know everything. I had no doubt that he knew why both Denny and Gettig had been killed. I was even sure—now that he'd been here—that he knew why Kenneth Martin had disappeared. I checked my watch. In less than two hours I would meet Stokes in his office. I didn't plan to leave without a lot of answers.

I stood up.

"I'm sorry if this has been painful for you, Mrs. Kubek."

The tears were back. "I just wish they'd find him, is all."

"Maybe they will," I said.

With a deadness that startled me, she said, "That ain't how things turn out for me, mister."

TWENTY-TWO

On the way back downtown, Cindy said, "You're pretty quiet for a compulsive talker."

Under other circumstances, that line would have struck me as very funny. At the moment it did nothing for me at all. "I'm having one of my great moments of doubt. I can see the possibility that Kenneth Martin had something to do with the Amis robbery. But I don't know what that would have to do with the deaths of Denny and Gettig. And I sure can't figure out how your husband would come into possession of Martin's bag."

"Maybe when we talk to Stokes tonight—"

I looked at her. "We?"

"Sure. We. I mean, I hope you're not planning to dump me now. It's kind of late in the game." She was joking but there was an anxiety in her voice. "I mean, that's something Clay would do. Not take me along."

What could I say? That I was going to be just like the husband who'd mistreated her over the years?

We spent the hour and a half waiting to go to Stokes's in a tiny bar meant to be intimate but that succeeded only in being oppressive. Peanut shells crunched underfoot like broken glass and the jukebox threatened to deafen you. Photos of NFL players looked down at us with the reverence of saints.

"May I ask you a question?" Cindy said after our second drink.

"Sure."

"Maybe you won't want to answer it."

"That bad, huh?"

"It's about your first wife."

"Oh-oh."

"Why she left you, I mean."

I smiled. "It was probably for all the right reasons." I shrugged. "I'm not exactly a prize, you know."

"You're a prize to me."

"You don't know me well enough yet."

"What a great self-image."

"Just what I love. Pop-psychology jargon."

"Some of it's true."

"Some of it."

"How about one more question?"

"What?"

"When I asked you about wanting to get married again, were you serious?"

"Very."

She smiled again. "Good."

I glanced at my watch and thought of Hauser, my accountant. He had been supposed to call me back. Tough to do when I'd left the office early. I wondered if what he had to say would have any bearing on my meeting with Stokes.

I explained all this to Cindy, then got up and worked my way back to the phone. It would have helped if I'd been a lineman for the Packers.

Then it was a ten-minute wait while a slickie in a toupee pleaded with his secretary to let him come over to her apartment. He sounded horny and lonely and pathetic all at the same time. I had begun to feel sorry for him until—getting me off the hook—he glanced up at me in the middle of a plaintive sentence and winked at me. Mr. Sincerity.

Finally, he took his lies and his middle-aged lust and his toupee back to the bar.

My accountant, Hauser, did well enough to live in the second most prestigious section of the city. His wife had the right kind of voice for the address, too, a cultured tone with just a hint of proper sexuality.

Hauser, when he came on the phone, struggled to sound happy to hear from me. "Hey," he said, "good to hear from you."

"Hey, yourself," I said. "I wondered if you'd figured out anything yet."

"Matter of fact, I have."

He paused long enough for a drumroll. Finally, he said, "Your accountant, Wickes, and your partner, Harris, were defrauding you."

Though that's about what I'd expected to hear, I still felt shock and anger. There's a difference between suspecting your wife of being unfaithful and walking in on her.

"The Eagle Production angle," Hauser went on. "Clay Traynor was involved, too. Your company billed Traynor's company for very expensive commercials that never actually got shot, then when Traynor paid your company, I think there was a three-way split. Eagle was a dummy company that Harris and Wickes set up."

I swore.

"Unfortunately," he said, "that's not all."

"Great."

"I'm not quite sure how to tell you this."

"Flat out is the best way."

"Your company is about three weeks away from bankruptcy."

This time I swore for a long time. Hauser had the good grace to let me go on.

138

"Harris and Wickes," he said, "they were embezzling the profits from the Eagle setup—and they were embezzling the regular company profits, too, and investing them in a variety of ways. Wickes is not what I'd consider an investment genius." Now it was his turn to swear. "Up until a few months ago, they managed to hide what they were doing. Then the losses got too great."

A guy had come up to stand outside the phone booth. He held a drink in his hand. A drink I needed much worse than he did. I opened the door a bit and pointed at his glass. "I'll give you ten dollars for your drink."

"You kidding, buddy?"

"I wish I were."

He studied me a moment. "That must be one helluva bad phone call."

I didn't have time to explain the real situation so I used shorthand, something simple and powerful. "How would you feel if your wife suddenly told you she was in love with another man?"

He handed me the drink and disappeared without asking for my ten-dollar bill.

On the other end of the phone Hauser was chuckling. "You advertising people are damned clever."

"Yeah," I said, "you can ask my dead partner just how clever." Then I had to ask. Had to. "Is there any way I can turn my financial position around?"

His pause said everything. "I don't think so, Michael. I really don't. Wickes has managed to stave off the worst of your creditors by giving them partial payments—but that's only going to last a few weeks longer."

"Let me ask you something and I'd appreciate a straight answer."

"Sure," he said, sounding a bit apprehensive.

"Denny Harris and Merle Wickes—given the situation

they were in, do you think they'd be capable of pulling off a robbery?"

"Straight answer, right?"

"Right."

"I knew Denny for over ten years and he was a totally charming guy, lots of fun to be around. But he was also completely unscrupulous. I wouldn't put anything past him. And Merle—well, he's just this pathetic little guy who Denny pumped up into believing he was a big man. Merle would go along with anything that Denny wanted to do. And obviously he did. I doubt that Merle would have had courage enough to become an embezzler without Denny there to hold his hand."

"Yeah, I doubt it, too."

Hauser yawned.

"I'm sorry I called so late," I said.

"It's all right," he said. "Actually, I'm glad it's over with, giving you the bad news, I mean."

"Thanks," I said.

"You'll need to sit down with me and we'll have to figure out how you start a new agency."

"Yeah," I said. Numbness was starting to set in. All I could think of was Hauser's response to my question—that Denny was capable of anything.

I thought of the missing guard Kenneth Martin—and of the robbery of hundreds of thousands of dollars in gems—and of two murders.

Then I thought of the private eye named Stokes, whom I'd be seeing in less than a half hour.

Many things were starting to come clear in my mind.

Too many things.

"Thanks, again," I said.

He sighed. "I'm sorry, Michael."

"Yeah," I said, and hung up.

TWENTY-THREE

On the way over to Stokes's I told Cindy everything I'd learned. Everything. Even about her husband.

"God," she said. Then she fell silent, watching the cold night shadows move across the moonlit snow and the tiny houses huddled against the universe.

"I'm sorry," I said. "I shouldn't have told you. A friend of mine told me once—beware people who are eager to give you bad news."

She sighed. "I suspected something, anyway. After you told me about the robbery I started thinking about certain signs over the last year—things started disappearing from our house, silver sets, jewelry, things like that. Clay has always lived beyond his means. I knew we'd have to pay for it some-day." She shook her head obstinately, with a sadness as weary as the widow Kubek's had been.

"His cousin can help him out."

"I don't think so, Michael. He's not the type to help any-body out. I just want it over with," she said. "Everything. I want to know who murdered Denny and Gettig, and I want to know why. Then I want the police to do their job and take the killer away—and then I want . . ." She paused. "And then I want you and me to try and make sense of things with each other. Don't you?"

"You bet I do."

Then she turned back to the passing silence and her brooding again.

Half a block from Stokes's home I saw the running man. He came out of shadows so deep he was virtually one with them. At first my headlights caught only a glimpse of him. Then he ran into their ken, light and snow illuminating his bloody face and hands.

Even through the black overcoat, you could see blood seeping and soaking.

His glasses were on his eyes but they had been smashed. He was running blind, his arms flailing, his feet slipping on wet pavement.

He slammed into the car of his own volition then rolled away to the side.

Cindy screamed.

I braked, skidding, fighting the wheel for control.

I slid into a curbing, then up over to icy grass. My car came to a halt a few feet from a big maple tree.

Cindy's breath came in gasps.

I said nothing, just ripped the door open and worked my way out of the car, careful to put my feet down deliberately so I didn't slip.

A concussion wouldn't help me find out what was going on.

Moans came from somewhere down the street. I moved toward a black bulk on the edge of a street light's circle of illumination.

Stokes was there. Waiting. Dying.

He had started to vomit thick clots of blood. To stop himself from choking he'd rolled over on his side.

As I got near him, he reacted instinctively and began feeling inside his black overcoat for his pistol.

Whoever had shot him had taken it from him.

Stokes was grasping for nothing.

He started to sit up, looking wildly as if he were going to run.

I knew I should have had more compassion—he was still a human being even if he was a damned mercenary version of one—but I couldn't help myself. I didn't want him to get up, I didn't want to have to chase him. He had only a few breaths left and I wanted him to spend them explaining to me what was going on.

I kicked him in the side. Not so hard that I broke anything. But not so gently that he'd think I was a good buddy, either.

Then I knelt down and grabbed his jaw so that he couldn't avoid my face.

"Who shot you, Stokes?" I said.

He couldn't see because of his smashed glasses. His hands flailed and groped in front of me. I twisted one of his wrists then slammed his arm to his chest.

"Who shot you, Stokes?" I repeated.

From behind me I heard a scream.

Cindy had come up, seen what I was doing.

"Please, Michael," she said, trying to calm me down. "Can't you see what condition he's in?"

I turned back to Stokes. "Now I know why you black-mailed Merle Wickes, why you said he had access to money. It was my company's money he had access to, wasn't it? You thought he'd pay you off to keep you from telling me about the embezzlement."

He had started choking on his own blood again.

Cindy grabbed me. "Is there anything we can do?" she cried.

I shook her away. "Then you came to me to tell me that Denny was having an affair with Cindy so I'd pay you to investigate him. Only then you stumbled on to something much bigger—the robbery that Denny and Merle and Gettig

143

were in on together. Then you really had something to blackmail them with—but you didn't count on the killer. Something went wrong. A guard named Kenneth Martin disappeared and the people involved in the robbery started getting murdered. The killer even managed to get around to you, didn't he?"

I don't know when I realized it, but eventually I saw that my words were useless. Stokes was dead.

I looked down at him. Part of his face was dark red from blood. The other part was white from frost. His blind eyes stared up at me.

"You scared me, Michael, the way you looked and sounded—"

"I'm sorry," I said. Then I grabbed her and buried my face in her shoulder.

TWENTY-FOUR

The back seat of Bonnell's police vehicle was surprisingly warm. He'd even been thoughtful enough to bring along a thermos filled with coffee.

He sat in the front seat, only turned around so he could face both Cindy and me.

In the windshield behind him I could see the emergency lights from the ambulance and the police vehicles splashing bloody light over the sullen neighborhood.

"I don't expect there are going to be many people at Mr. Stokes's funeral," Detective Bonnell said. "Not unless they turn out to gloat."

"I need to talk to you," I said.

"I hope you're ready to tell me the truth," he said.

"I am."

I told him everything about the murders I'd learned to date. Everything—from the embezzlement to the robbery to the disappearance of the security guard named Kenneth Martin. Then I told him about lying for Clay to give him an alibi.

Bonnell stared at me. "Somehow you don't strike me as the type to lie."

"I thought of my father in the nursing home. He was an

honest man. He would want his son to be. I just want the killer stopped."

Cindy took my hand, squeezed it.

Bonnell said, "I ran a check on Stokes. He was not a licensed investigator—he couldn't have been with his police record, which was long and formidable and included convictions for extortion, rape, and armed robbery."

Cindy leaned forward. "You don't still think my husband committed the murders, do you?" she asked.

He frowned, a curious expression filling his chunky face. He looked at me, then slowly—almost unwillingly—at Cindy.

"No, I don't think your husband is who we've been looking for, Mrs. Traynor." He glanced up at me, then back to Cindy. "Your husband's dead, Mrs. Traynor. Somebody murdered him earlier this evening."

Ten minutes later, the ambulance driver slid in the back seat where I'd been and handed Cindy a sedative.

She was not doing well. Her first reaction had been tears, but she'd slid immediately into a terrible frozen state that was frightening to watch. Shock, the ambulance driver said.

Bonnell and I stood outside the car, our breath pluming the night air, several Action News types looking longingly at us—as if our conversation would be the most interesting anywhere in the world if only they could eavesdrop.

"You got any ideas about what's going on?" I asked.

"Only one. The guard."

"Kenneth Martin?"

He nodded. "It's obvious Martin was involved in the robbery with them. But since we don't know what happened, I guess it's fair to do a little speculating. What if Martin were paying each of them back?"

"For what?"

"For double-crossing him. From what you've told me about your partner, Harris, he certainly sounds capable of

146

that. But what would happen if they cheated Martin out of his share of the robbery proceeds, maybe even tried to kill him, only somehow he managed to escape and has spent his time since then killing them one by one? There's no motive as powerful as vengeance."

"But why would he kill Stokes?"

Bonnell shrugged. "Simple enough. Stokes figured out who was doing it. Given Stokes's tendencies, he may even have tried to blackmail Martin. So Martin kills him."

He followed the line of my eyes. The last few minutes of the conversation I hadn't heard totally. I'd been watching Cindy deal with her grief over Clay.

"Nice lady," he said.

"Yeah."

"You should take care of her."

"I know," I said, turning back to him. I stared at him a moment. "It isn't over yet, is it?"

"No," he said flatly.

"What happens now?"

"We put out an APB on Mr. Martin, and probably we have a long talk with Mr. Wickes."

"You think he can help?"

"Right now, he knows more about the robbery than anybody who's alive—except for Mr. Martin, of course. Even though he wasn't directly involved in it—which is why he's alive, apparently—he knows all the people and what happened to the gems."

"Yeah, I keep forgetting about the gems. I guess murder has a way of distracting my attention."

"Somewhere there's a lot of money in gems. Presumably Mr. Martin can tell us when we find him."

The ambulance driver got out of the back of Bonnell's car.

I started toward Cindy. I needed badly to see her, touch her, even if only to hold her hand.

Bonnell stopped me.

147

"There aren't any heroes in this," he said.

"I know."

"But I'm glad you told me the truth."

"So am I."

He nodded to his car. "Go take Mrs. Traynor home. She should probably stay at your place tonight."

"Thanks."

"Good night, Mr. Ketchum."

He let me precede him to the car. I opened the door and put my hand inside for Cindy to take. There was nothing to say. I held my hand there, feeling cold and tired and scared.

Finally she took my hand.

"We should go home," I said.

"Home?" she said.

"My place."

She leaned over and kissed me. "Home. That sounds good."

TWENTY-FIVE

My place looked as dark as Denny's had the night I'd found him dead. I almost didn't want to leave the car. Cindy had fallen asleep with her head on my shoulder.

I raised her face gently and kissed her and then we started out into the night, her sleepy as a wakened child.

"I love you," I said, and kissed her.

I got the apartment door open and pushed it in and stood back to let her precede me. It was then that I caught my first glimpse of Merle Wickes and the gun he was holding. It looked to be the same gun he was fondling the day before when he'd apparently been contemplating suicide.

"Clay's dead," he said. Merle had been waiting in the dark. I found the switch and turned the overhead on.

"You mind if I put her to bed?" I said.

By this time, the sedative having taken effect, Cindy didn't seem even slightly aware of Merle's presence. I had plopped her down on the couch, where she sat now zombielike, staring straight ahead.

Merle smiled nastily. "You like fucking dead men's wives?"

"You like walking around without any teeth?"

Even with the gun, Merle was not a brave man in the face of real anger.

In the bedroom, I pulled back the cover, then began stripping Cindy to her underwear. I clicked on the electric blanket and pushed her fondly beneath the sheets. I stood staring at her a long moment, loving her.

Merle was pacing when I got back to the living room. He was so caught up in his thoughts he didn't hear me come up from behind him. He looked silly with his lounge-singer hairdo and the gun dangling from his slender fingers.

"Thanks for ruining my company," I said.

I pushed him hard and he went crashing into an end table, slamming his knee hard and crying out in a high voice.

"You're on the hook for an embezzlement rap, Merle, and I'm going to make damned sure that charges are pressed." I glared down at him, still angry. "You can't do anything right, Merle. You can't even have a mistress. Clay was sleeping with her." I laughed. "You're a wimp, Merle, and I'm about to prove it."

"What's that mean?" he said petulantly.

I walked over to him. He raised the gun as if to hold me at bay, but he did absolutely nothing when I reached down and took it from him.

"It means," I said, "that the police are looking for you right now. But before I call them I want to know where Kenneth Martin is."

"Kenneth Martin? You're crazy."

"The guard, Merle, the guard who helped Clay and Denny and Gettig steal Mrs. Amis's gems."

Merle seemed to swell up momentarily. Cockiness shone in his eyes. He took himself out of his slouch and laughed. "You think you've got this all figured out, don't you?"

"I've got it figured out enough that I know Kenneth Martin is killing people because they double-crossed him."

150

"Kenneth Martin is dead, you moron. I saw him myself—where they buried him after they shot him."

All I could do was stare at him. "Then who the hell is doing the killings?"

"I don't know."

"Bull," I said.

"Look, if I knew, don't you think I'd tell you? There's a good chance whoever it is wants to kill me next. That's why I'm here. I'd hoped maybe you'd figured things out." Now he was the more familiar Merle. Pleading. Wimpy.

"Get out of here, Merle," I said.

"God," he said, "this is a good place to hide." He was desperate now. "Please. Please, Michael."

"Get out, Merle."

"Whoever it is, he'll kill me."

"Maybe that'll be better than prison. That's where you're headed, Merle, and you're not tough enough to survive."

"God, Michael, you were always a decent guy before."

"Yeah," I snapped. "and look where it got me. I've been embezzled out of a business and I'm stuck in the middle of murders I had nothing to do with."

"Please, Michael. Please let me stay."

I raised the gun and aimed it dead center in the middle of his face. "I wouldn't push your luck, Merle."

All he said was, "Maybe I'll turn myself over."

I said nothing.

"Well," he said, as if he were starting a sentence. But it was a sentence he never finished.

He could see I didn't want to talk.

He left.

An hour later I was knocking back my third bourbon, hoping to kill the anxiety enough so that I could lie back on the couch and sleep.

I turned the light out and closed my eyes and felt a sudden torpor rush through me. I felt old and used up and very, very unwise. I thought of Merle out there, running, terrified. He'd been our last best hope—the guy both Detective Bonnell and I thought could clear everything up. The guy who could lead us to Kenneth Martin.

Only Kenneth Martin was dead, killed by the three men who were themselves dead now.

The phone rang.

I sat there and stared at it as if I were a bush native and had never seen such a newfangled instrument.

Finally, maybe the tenth ring, I picked it up.

Even over the phone her weariness came through oppressively. The widow Kubek.

"Something is wrong," she said. "Somebody is in his room now. I'm scared."

"Call the police," I said.

"I can't, Mr. Ketchum. Maybe it's him. Maybe he's in trouble. I'd just be making the trouble worse if I called the police."

I didn't want to tell her. Couldn't. That I'd leave to the good grace and long experience of the police.

"I'll be right over," I said.

Before leaving, I checked on Cindy, then looked up Bonnell's name in the phone directory.

He hadn't been asleep, either. He sounded almost happy that I'd called him. I said I'd see him there.

TWENTY-SIX

I had no trouble breaking the speed limit. I didn't see a single patrol car in the entire eight-mile trip. Only the ghostly flash of yellow stoplights against the dawning sky.

Bonnell's car was waiting when I arrived.

He put out a surprisingly friendly hand when I walked up the stairs and met him in front of the room where Kenneth Martin had lived.

Mrs. Kubek was there, too, wrapped inside a frayed and faded housecoat, looking frail and old. Only her rage animated her face. She glowered at me as I greeted Bonnell.

"I didn't want the cops called," she snapped. "I didn't want any trouble."

"Mrs. Kubek—" I said, about to explain that her lover was dead and was beyond the grasp of earthly trouble. But then I stopped myself. "You don't know who was here tonight?"

"It wasn't Kenneth," she said.

I looked at Bonnell. "You think we could speak alone?"

"Sure," he said. He turned to Mrs. Kubek. "Maybe we'll talk in Mr. Martin's room, if you don't mind, Mrs. Kubek."

"He didn't do nothing wrong, Kenneth. He didn't."

"I'm sure he didn't," Bonnell said, soothing as a country priest.

She had one more laserlike glower left for me. Then she left.

We went inside. I closed the door and said, "Martin's dead."

"What?" Bonnell said, surprised as I'd been.

I told him about Merle Wickes's visit.

"Damn," Bonnell said. "Then who's been doing all the killing?"

I couldn't help myself. I found his question amusing. "I thought you were the cop, not me."

He smiled. "Yeah, I see what you mean."

I looked around the room, at its cleanliness and orderliness. It was a testament to Kenneth Martin's determination to lead a civilized life even if he had to do it in bad conditions.

"Reminds me of my uncle's room," Bonnell said. "He was a railroad man, lifelong bachelor. I used to come up and visit him. Since he didn't have any kids of his own, he always had plenty of money to spend on me."

I thought of Martin's little nephew in the photograph I'd seen the other day. Martin probably would have had his nephew visit him, too—if the nephew and his parents hadn't been killed in a car accident.

Bonnell sat down in a straight-back chair. "You think it might have been Wickes here tonight?"

"I don't think Merle could have driven from my place to here in time."

Bonnell frowned, studied aspects of the room some more. "Not much here that's helpful."

He stood up, started walking around. I watched him, then leaned back on the edge of the bed and looked at the photo of Martin in his Korean uniform.

"This sure would have been an easy case if Martin had only had the courtesy to stay alive," Bonnell said ruefully.

"Yeah, wouldn't it."

154

Bonnell thumbed through Martin's pipe collection. "I wonder why somebody would have come here tonight."

"Maybe the gems."

He shook his head. "No. If it was the gems they were after, they would have been here a long time ago and tossed the room. Nobody's done that." He sounded very sure of himself. "The gems have been in the hands of the killer for a long time. Safe and sound." He got quizzical again. "So why would somebody be here tonight?"

A knock came on the door.

Bonnell went to open it.

Mrs. Kubek stood there, shuddering from the cold. "Just wondered if you were about done. I gotta get up in a few hours. I need my sleep."

Bonnell shrugged. "Just a few more minutes."

She glowered at me just once then turned to walk back down the stairs.

I raised my eyes to the photograph of Martin again and then to the Mitchell Junior College pennant next to it.

I got fixated on the pennant without quite knowing why, just staring at its green and yellow colors until gradually the wrongness of it struck me.

"Why would he have a junior-college pennant?"

"What?" Bonnell said.

"Why would a man in his fifties have a junior-college pennant?" Otherwise this was a somber room, nothing frivolous.

"Maybe his niece or nephew went there."

"He only had a nephew and he died in a car accident with his parents."

Bonnell shrugged. "Maybe he followed the football team. Mitchell's got a good junior varsity squad."

I shrugged, thinking maybe he was right but not quite believing him.

"Well," he said, "no sense in making Mrs. Kubek any angrier. Might as well leave."

"Yeah," I said.

I stood up, looked around the room, followed Bonnell out. He closed the door and it clicked shut with a real finality.

"I wish I knew what the hell was going on," he said. There was a genuine sadness in his voice.

As we passed by the office on the way to our cars, I saw Mrs. Kubek standing in the shadows. Obviously she hoped we didn't see her.

"Just a minute," I said.

Bonnell nodded. "I need to tell Mrs. Kubek about Martin."

"Can I ask her a question first?" I said.

I walked up to the office door and turned the handle. It was locked.

From the shadows Mrs. Kubek stared at me. She made no move to open the door.

"Mrs. Kubek," I said, "I need to ask you a question."

"Go away," she said.

"Mrs. Kubek," I said. "Please." I wondered if I sounded as whiny as Merle Wickes had at my place.

The door opened.

"You stay there," she said. "What's your question?"

"The Mitchell Junior College pennant in Kenneth's room. Why did he have it?"

"That's your question?" she snapped. "It's a stupid one."

"What's the answer, Mrs. Kubek?"

"Because his nephew went there."

"The little boy in the photograph?"

"Yes."

"You told me he was dead."

"You don't hear too good, Mr. Ketchum. What I said was the mother and father died. The boy, he lived in an orphanage. He came up to see Kenneth all the time. They love each other like father and son."

I looked at Bonnell, as a terrible idea came to mind.

156

"Do you have a picture of this boy?" I asked.

"Sure," she said.

"I need to see it," I said.

"Can't it wait till tomorrow?"

"No, it can't, Mrs. Kubek. It really can't."

"What's wrong?" Bonnell asked me when Mrs. Kubek shuffled away to get the photograph.

"It's starting to make sense," I said.

"What is?" Bonnell said.

"Who the killer is?"

"It is?" Bonnell asked.

"The only person it could be. The only person young enough to go to a junior college."

"What are you talking about?"

I had to put it together in my mind before I could say it. Three months ago somebody had started work at my agency. This was just after Martin had disappeared. Those two facts could have been coincidence until you considered that the murders had started soon after. Then coincidence became hard to explain—especially when you began to realize that with his agency job my new employee knew a great deal about our comings and goings. He would know, with his special vantage point, when to strike out.

"I wish I knew what the hell you were talking about," Bonnell said.

Mrs. Kubek came back and handed me a Polaroid photo, which I angled into the light.

"Meet Tommy Byrnes," I said to Bonnell, giving him the picture.

Then Bonnell proceeded to tell her about Martin's death.

TWENTY-SEVEN

One minute later I was using Mrs. Kubek's phone. But to no avail.

Either Cindy was still unconscious from the sedative, or . . .

I didn't like to think of "or." But it was obvious that Tommy Byrnes meant to get each of us in repayment for the death of his uncle.

I slammed the phone and asked Bonnell if he had a siren on his car.

I didn't even give him time to say yes. I just pushed him toward his Pontiac.

I had left home so quickly I hadn't noticed the red Mazda at the far end of my parking lot.

As Bonnell's headlights swept over the cars in the lot, I noticed the red vehicle and realized whose it was.

Merle Wickes's.

I was out of the Pontiac, running, before Bonnell had fully stopped.

I slipped on the ice as I ran toward the car, banged my knee against the pavement, swore, but kept running.

I skidded over to the Mazda, glanced inside, then quickly glanced away.

I had never seen anything like it. In the average experience of the average man, seeing a person with his throat cut is not a common experience.

Tommy had found Merle with no problem. I looked in once again, only to confirm the horrible image that had been pressed on my eyes moments before. Merle was still in there, his throat slashed—his hair, ironically, in perfect composure.

Behind me, Bonnell was saying something, but I didn't hear the exact words.

I was already on my way up the stairs.

Terrified that I was too late.

I reached for the banister to help my flight be faster. Something sticky clung to my palm. I knew what it was without looking. I moved two steps at a time now.

My apartment door was slightly ajar when I reached it, the crack between door and frame dark.

I stopped, not out of fear for myself but afraid that Tommy might not have hurt her—and that my sudden presence might panic him into doing so.

My breathing crashed in my ears—I was dripping with sweat and freezing at the same time—as I eased up to the door and put my fingers on it.

I could hear Bonnell thundering into the vestibule below.

I pushed the door open and went in.

In the moonlight through the large living-room window, I saw him.

He stood silhouetted in the window, facing me, leaning against the ledge as if he were perfectly relaxed.

He held a gun and it was aimed directly at me.

"You're too late," he said. "She's dead."

His statement stopped me completely. Rage, disbelief, the first wave of shock—all moved through me at the same time.

I would have lunged at him, unafraid of his weapon, but I had no strength.

All I could do was stand and breathe and try to collect my thoughts into something coherent—but something that did not face what he'd just told me.

"You killed him," he said.

"I didn't," I said after a time. "I didn't have anything to do with it. Neither did Cindy."

"Just by being who you are, you killed him," Tommy said. "Your kind of people . . ." There was a rage in his voice that matched the rage in my heart. "They blackmailed him into helping with the robbery. They'd found out about a drunk driving rap he'd had one time—they threatened to tell his bosses."

Tommy had started crying.

"I'm sorry, Tommy," I said, and I was.

"He was the only thing that kept me going in the orphanage," Tommy said. "He would've taken me if he could've afforded it."

"I'm sure he was a good man, Tommy," I said. Then I thought of Cindy and my pity for him waned.

I wanted to kick him as I'd kicked Stokes earlier tonight. Only Tommy I wanted to kick to death.

"It doesn't matter anymore," Tommy said, "who lives or who dies. It just doesn't matter."

In silhouette I could see him raise the gun. I heard the safety come off.

I gathered myself enough to stall him a little.

"Another killing," I said.

"Like I said, it doesn't matter. It didn't matter to them about my uncle. They killed him, anyway."

"Tommy—"

He raised the gun.

It happened so quickly I scarcely realized what he'd done.

Turn the weapon on himself. Directly to his forehead. Squeeze the trigger.

Once.

Which was more than enough.

TWENTY-EIGHT

I was in the bedroom by the time Tommy had fallen to the floor. There was nothing I could do for him, anyway.

Cindy was sprawled on the bed.

There was no sign of blood. But neither was there any sign of breathing.

I got the table light on and saw immediately that he'd strangled her. Probably he hadn't wanted to waken the neighbors with gunshots.

Bonnell pounded into the room.

"Let me," he said, rushing over.

But I couldn't let go of her. I held on to her as if we would be embracing that way for eternity.

Bonnell wasn't impressed.

He wanted to help her, if that was still possible.

I can't ever recall being hit so hard in my life. He knocked me unconscious in a single punch.

Four hours later the young intern in the white smock signaled that I could go into the room. He held up three fingers—the three minutes I'd agreed to.

The window was smudged with overcast morning light. In her hospital bed she looked very white and very frail. I went over to her side and started to lean down and kiss her when her eyes came open.

"Hi," she said, after bringing me into focus.

I sighed. It was great to hear her talk. She could have read the phone book and I would have been delighted.

"Hi," I said back.

"I guess it all got resolved, didn't it?"

"Yeah."

"Poor Tommy. Before he started choking me, he told me about himself. I can't help it, I feel sorry for him."

I thought of Tommy the last way I'd seen him—virtually without a head. "Yeah," I said, "poor Tommy."

She smiled up at me. "You still thinking about giving up your bachelor status?"

I smiled back. "Thinking about it, yes." Then I said, "Last night, when I was helping you up the steps to my apartment, I told you that I loved you."

"I hope I had the grace to be appreciative." She reached out her hand. "I love you too, Michael."

An intern came in looking very serious.

"I'll be back tonight," I said to Cindy.

"You'd better be," she said.

I leaned over and kissed her on the cheek and left. She was dozing off before I got out the door.

Bonnell was in the lobby.

"I figured I'd find you here," he said.

"I have to fill out evidence forms or something?" I said.

"Not that I know of. It's wrapped up. We found the gems in Denny Harris's basement." He smiled. "Just thought I'd buy us both a little breakfast. My wife hates cooking, so I thought I'd do her a favor and eat out."

"Sounds great," I said.

I paused, looking back at the room.

"Nothing's ever easy, is it?" I said, thinking of the last few days, then thinking of Cindy.

"Nothing worth having," he said, leading the way down the hall to the elevators.

162